AMAZON ... AUTHOR

THE DEVIL'S SUITCASE

FRANCIS JOSEPH SMITH

THE DEVIL'S SUITCASE

BY

FRANCIS JOSEPH SMITH

Second printing

PUBLISHED BY AMAZON

www.amazon.com

Printed in the United States of America

Also by Francis Joseph Smith:

THE VATICAN'S LAST SECRET

To my wife, daughter and son

"Now I am become Death, the destroyer of worlds."

Bhagavad Gita

"If you make a deal with the devil, he is going to want his cut."

FJS

PROLOGUE

Washington DC - Capitol - Present Day

The senior congresswoman from Pennsylvania anxiously tapped the senate podium's angled microphone, verifying its acoustics for the third time. Looking about the room as she absently shuffled her notes, amazed at the full turnout on only an hour's notice. She had come straight from the White House after her one-on-one meeting with the President—*a meeting where he had clearly threatened her life.*

Of course, he had requested the Oval Office to be cleared prior to their meeting. He wanted no witnesses, not even his ever-present Secret Service agent.

She had to take the Presidents threat seriously due to his former directorship at the CIA. The bastard was even audacious enough to say that she would be signing her own death warrant if she went public with her claims.

Her own death warrant, she muttered under her breath. She had to admit it wasn't the first death threat she had received but definitely her first from a sitting United States president.

Eye contact with her husband in the visitor's section provided some sense of reassurance via his boyish smile. She mustered a slight nod in response.

"Ladies and gentlemen of the worldwide press," she said nervously. "I would like to thank-you for attending my impromptu news conference. As I stand here today it is with a heavy heart that I disclose certain facts to you, facts so sensational that the governments of both Russia and the United States will ardently deny what I am about to tell you."

She looked down at her notes but the print seemed out of focus. "Excuse me," she said as she removed a small pair of wire rimmed reading glasses from her jacket pocket, "but like some of you here, I'm just getting old."

A chorus of laughs greeted her.

She smiled before continuing. "Several months ago, I had the privilege of meeting with General Alexander Lebed, the onetime head of the Russian Department of Defense. I will not bore you with all of the details, but it was during a low point in our meeting that General Lebed excused himself from the table, motioning for me to follow suit. Once out of earshot, he proceeded to inform me of something his Government would ardently deny, and will still deny to this day." In disgust, the congresswoman suddenly pushed aside her notes, the words already burned into her memory. She cast a nervous glance towards her husband. He smiled once more in return. She turned to the assembled reporters only to be greeted by the look of uninterested expressions upon their faces.

Little did they know that in the next minute or so she was about to become one of the most prominent woman in the world, and the very reporters that now sat bored before her would make it all occur.

She continued. "The General realized the treacherous position he faced, willingly discussing a subject only nine people in his government were even cognizant of. He had a genuine look of dread about him as he uttered the words that have kept me wide-awake each night since our meeting: '*Russian authorities cannot account for dozens of portable nuclear weapons that are thought to be lost somewhere in the United States of America.*' "

The audience gasped.

Reporters anxiously reached for their cell phones, pleading for airtime. In their ever-changing world, a new top story had been crowned.

In the visitors' gallery, Lawrence Trevers straightened his United States Capitol Police officer's uniform, only minutes removed from its original owner. He moved easily among the tourists as he searched for just the right position to accomplish his mission. His high and tight haircut, lean body, and quick, darting eye movements betrayed that his identity lay somewhere else, another employer.

Originally instructed to be in position *before* the congresswoman's speech, a traffic jam in DuPont Circle put an end to that notion.

She had their undivided attention, of this, she was sure. "After our impromptu meeting, I waited until the initial shock wore off before approaching Defense Minister Pavel Sergeivich for confirmation. I simply wanted him to state that my source had been misinformed. His silence confirmed my worst fears. Minister Sergeivich went on to inform me that such devices did exist, and that yes, they are indeed missing in the United States."

The room came alive once more, reporters rapidly firing question after question as they each sought the congresswoman's attention.

Trevers circled to the rear of the visiting crowd. Satisfied no one was watching him—he screwed a bulbous silencer into the tip of his 9mm before placing it back into his jacket pocket.

No one took notice as he maneuvered into shooting position, looking perfectly normal to anyone who happened to glance in his direction.

The congresswoman continued. "Minister Sergeivich said he would never officially repeat his remarks. He considered his words strictly off the record. Unfortunately, Minister Sergeivich was a man of his word. Within two weeks of our discussion, he was dead. The Official Russian version of the story is that he apparently surprised a burglar in his home. However, according to my sources, the FSB, the KGB's heir apparent, are the prime suspects in his death."

She paused for a moment, the stress of the past several weeks evidently weighing on her. "As for General Lebed, an assassin's bullet found him two days ago while attending a veteran's reunion. The same crooked finger pointing back to the FSB. It doesn't take a rocket scientist to see who is behind this." She maintained eye contact with her audience as she placed her notes in her jacket pocket. "I thank-you all for coming. More statements will be forthcoming from my office over the course of the next several days."

As the Congresswoman walked from the podium, reporters shouted questions at breakneck speed, probing for additional details, only to have her casually wave them off.

Crossing before the Senate Master at Arms chair, a red dot suddenly appeared on her forehead.

The bullet had clearly hit its target.

Several days following the congresswoman's funeral, Russian officials issued a formal statement denying they had fielded such weapons, widely denouncing the United States.

In a closed-door meeting, a highly placed United States official admitted to a New York Times reporter that the Soviet Union had indeed placed nuclear devices in the United States. The Official also went on to state that all of the weapons had been accounted for and dismantled by a joint US-Russian team.

Someone was lying.................

CHAPTER ONE

Berlin – 22 April 1945

Adolf Hitler shuffled into his underground bunker corridor half bent, his left arm shaking uncontrollably. Although he was 5 foot 8 inches tall, now, with his head and body twisted to the left, he looked much smaller. The eyes that his admirers had once called "magnetic" were feverish and red, as if he had not slept for days. His face was puffy, and its color was a blotchy, faded gray. A pair of pale green glasses hung from his right hand; bright light bothered him now. For a moment he gazed expressionlessly at his generals as their hands shot up and out to a chorus of *"Heil Hitler."*

The corridor was so crowded that Hitler had some difficulty getting past everyone to reach the bunkers small conference room. Slowly, as though in pain, Hitler scuffled to his place at the head of the table. He motioned for those about him to sit before turning to the colorful maps that lay spread out on the table in front of him. He managed a slight smile as he anxiously tapped the maps of his ever-shrinking empire.

His hands trembled as he shuffled his notes, deciding it best to lay them on the table. He knew the Russian Army were at the very edge of Berlin itself. As he was about to speak, there was a loud uproar in the hall and the immense bulk of Hermann Goering suddenly filled the doorway of the little conference room. Pushing his way in, Goering heartily greeted those present, shaking Hitler's hand enthusiastically as he excused himself for being late.

Goering then addressed Hitler in a loud voice so all present could hear his news: "My Fuhrer," he began, "What you have asked of me a fortnight ago has been accomplished." He smiled about the room as if a child who had just pleased his parents.

Hitler suddenly sprang to life. He pounded on the table in front of him. "Faith!" he yelled. "Faith and a strong belief in success will make up for all of your inefficiencies!" He looked about the room as if 10 years younger than when he had entered. His face now crimson, the gray since vanished, his eyes vibrant once more. "Field Marshall Goering has brought me the best news of the war." He turned to his generals assembled about the small table. "I will tell you," he yelled, if you are conscious of the fact that this war should be won, it will be won! If your troops are given the same belief—then you will achieve victory, and the greatest success of the war!"

In the tense silence that followed, Hitler dismissed all about him but Goering, motioning for him to stay. Goering nodded before closing the room's door. Now, just the two of them stood face-to-face about an empty room.

Hitler took the seat at the head of the table; Goering took a chair beside him. It was remarkable the change in Hitler's health, if just for the moment.

"My Fuhrer," Goering began, "I can still have you flown out within the hour. We don't have long before the whole city is surrounded. You can go to Bavaria and personally bring the news to our engineers. They have been working for years to achieve this miracle. They only lacked the material to set the bomb in motion. In a matter of days they will have a working prototype ready for use against our enemies, one that could destroy whole cities with a single blast! It must be you, My Fuhrer!"

Hitler shook his head. "No," he said meekly, "I have made my decision to stay. I shall not leave Berlin. I will defend the city with my troops to the end. Either I will win the battle for our Reich's capital or I shall die as a symbol for the Reich."

Goering thought his decision was madness. "I must insist," he said to Hitler, "you must leave for Berchtesgaden within the hour."

Hitler refused to listen. "I want you to fly to Berchtesgaden, but not before our two guests arrive," he yelled at Goering, before leaving the room.

A ½ mile from the Bunker, along the East-West Axis—the broad highway running from the river Havel on the west to the Unter den Linden on the east—a plane suddenly swept in and landed, maneuvering up to the Brandenburg Gate. It was a small Fieseler Storch containing a pilot and a scientist. The two had been summoned to Berlin by Goering and Hitler.

Goering knocked once on the door leading into Hitler's private quarters before entering. As he entered he saw Hitler sitting in a chair facing a painting of Fredrick the Great; he was having a one-way conversation with the painting. He cleared his throat before announcing: "My Fuhrer, they have arrived!"

The young pilot and equally as young scientist were escorted into Hitler's private quarters. Hitler beamed as he gracefully shook first the scientists, and then the pilot's hand. "I have a mission for you that could help save Germany," he said before providing them the details. Ten minutes later, they were escorted back to their awaiting plane and a heavy metal suitcase was placed in its rear. "It's our new *Wonder Weapon,"* said the soldier in response to their disapproving looks.

Their plane never arrived at its Salzburg destination, shot down somewhere within the Soviet Army lines, its case disappearing for some 30 odd years..........

CHAPTER TWO

April 1975, Moscow, Soviet Union

A rain induced haze intermittently obscured the Kremlin's distinctive "onion dome" as the early morning showers moved obligingly from one unsuspecting area to yet another. This simple act of nature allowed the government complex to majestically appear in full view, presenting one with a sheer sense of awe when viewed from afar.

The streets were missing their normal traffic. With the upcoming May Day celebrations, many officials were settling in for a three-day weekend at one of their *dachas* outside the city limits.

The lone exception this night was a Soviet military truck that carefully weaved its way through Moscow's moonlit streets.

Lieutenant Yuri Stenko slowed his vehicle as he approached each turn not wanting to disturb his precious cargo nor his unit of six heavily armed Soviet Marines in the rear of the truck.

With their blue berets tilted to one side and AK-47's at the ready—they were the pride of the Soviet military.

The truck continued along a well-lit road that ran parallel to the Kremlin's red brick walls before slowing for the first set of security gates. Lieutenant Stenko smiled as he flashed his identification card at the heavily armed guard who approached him.

The immaculately dressed State Security Guard snapped to attention upon seeing the distinctive red-bordered identification card of a ranking Party Member, begging forgiveness for even stopping the Lieutenant's vehicle. The second guard swiftly followed suit, saluting and allowing the truck to proceed without the usual, thorough search.

As the truck rolled past the guards, a bolt of lightning streaked across the early morning sky as if announcing the trucks arrival to those below.

Cigarette smoke hung eerily in the air above the hand carved mahogany conference table as if it were an angel of death awaiting its cue before striking. Gathered around the table at this early morning hour were two of the most powerful men in the Soviet hierarchy; Soviet Premier Alexi Brezhnev and KGB Chief Luc Andropov. Both were of the same mold—tall, brooding, sadistic, and merciless in their actions. They rarely doled out rewards to their subordinates, mostly punishments for what they perceived as failure.

For several hours they had toasted to the departure of their American nemesis by drinking glass after glass of Vodka in celebration of Russian TV images showing the victorious Vietcong standing in the lobby of the American Embassy in Saigon.

Of course it didn't hurt that the Soviet government supplied most of the equipment and missiles to the North Vietnamese Military.

Alexi stood and raised his glass, gripping the table for support, feeling the impact from drinking almost half a liter of vodka. "To our Mother Russia, may she always counter the American swine in their quest for global domination," consuming the contents in one quick swallow.

Luc Andropov did the same. When finished, he proceeded to refill the Premiers glass, then his own. For a moment he stood contemplating his boss, pondering the possibly lethal step he was about to take. He felt the time was right to brief the Premier on his plan, one he had kept hidden for 4 long years. It was Luc's turn to raise his glass in celebration. "May we once again assume the role of superpower in the game of world domination with the Americans."

Both quickly consumed the vodka in their glass.

"Come, come, Comrade Andropov, we both know the Americans will win this marathon race we have endured for some 30 years—*allowing us to choke in their dust.* We will be forced to withdraw from the world stage in order to concentrate on more pressing matters within our own borders. Mark my words my friend, you will see."

Luc smiled shrewdly at the Premier, realizing he was correct in his belief—but only if the Soviet Union continued on its present course. Luc had greater ambitions for both himself and Mother Russia. On numerous occasions he had sought to broach the subject with the Premier but decided it best to wait until he had a working prototype. He had no desire to be exposed as some fool in front of his lifelong friend, a friend who controlled both the purse strings and the ability to crush his dreams.

Luc paused for a moment, reflecting back some 30 years to a time when they first met as political commissars, thrust together during the battle of Stalingrad. The savagery of the battle bonded them as no other single event could. After the war, their motivations pushed their careers onward and upward. Now they sat across from each other, both having risen to top positions in their government—only Alexi had progressed one-step further.

Focusing back on his friend, Luc realized the potential to solidify his position in the Communist Party, possibly even allowing the premier to recommend him when he chose to step down.

Pointing to the now empty vodka bottle, he laughed aloud before speaking. "Comrade Alexi, in our younger days we would polish off three or four of these and then the party would start in earnest. Dancing, caviar, women. Blondes, redheads, brunets! We had so many choices that you could pick the size, shape and color that you wanted," slamming his fist down on the table for emphasis. "Those were the days my friend."

Alexi could only nod in agreement. At his age, he was only thinking of his nice, comfortable, warm bed. Looking at his watch, he hoped to motivate Luc to speed his plans along.

Luc took notice, picking up the red phone at the center of the table, speaking rapidly before turning back to the Premier. "I have something I would like to show you, Comrade." He rose up from his leather chair and walked over to the conference room's main entrance. "This is a surprise for you, Alexi."

Leaning into the hallway, Luc focused on the officer in charge, beckoning him over. "Lieutenant, it is time." Luc held the door open to accommodate the marine who carried the one-meter by one and a half meter black suitcase, him followed by his fellow marines filing past, weapons at the ready.

The marine sergeant nervously eyed his lieutenant, then Luc, pondering where he should place the black case.

Luc realized the young man's dilemma, walking over to the sergeant and nodding as he relieved him of the lightweight case, choosing to place it directly in front of the premier.

Luc snapped open the cases five quick release latches as if a magician with a magic box. He intentionally chose not to remove the units cover—not wanting its contents to be revealed to anyone but the Premier.

"Lieutenant, you will station your men outside of each exit with yourself at the front door. If anyone tries to pass you or one of your guards, shoot to kill. Do you understand your orders? *Shoot to kill!*"

The Lieutenant nodded. "I understand, Comrade Andropov." Behind the lieutenant, his marine subordinates performed an about face, all following him out of the room.

Satisfied with the new security arrangements, Luc proceeded with part two of his carefully prepared plan, one that was four arduous years in the making. Luc stood over the suitcase as if a proud father about to debut his newborn child to the world. He reverently lifted the cover of the black suitcase before toggling the unit's power switch to the on position.

"Premier Brezhnev may I be the first to present an option to seize the moment and once again allow us to be on an equal footing with the Americans, quite possibly even allowing us to move ahead."

Alexi scanned the unit, taking in its complex dials and analog technology, obviously impressed with the manufacture of the unit. Alexi quickly accessed the situation, realizing the potential of the unit in front of him. He toggled the unit to the off position, allowing the gages to return to their dormant status.

"I can see why you have been busy avoiding my meetings for the past several months, Comrade Andropov. I see your small group of sequestered scientists at Rostov finally succeeded in producing the material for our Operation — *The Devils Suitcase.*"

A look of shock spread across Luc's face, him wondering how Alexi could have known about his closely guarded operation.

"Of course, I never thought we would actually get that Hitler prototype working," Alexi said, referring to the weapon they had discovered in the wreckage of an aircraft Russian forces had shot down in the closing days of WWII. "Sometimes I underestimate my own people."

Luc suddenly felt ill with the Premier's knowledge of his work at Rostov. Luc had taken extraordinary precautions, even eliminating the entire staff after the tests were completed. This would have left no one but himself with knowledge of the project. *That was until now.* He gripped the edge of the table for support as his mind raced.

"You look pale, my friend. Maybe the vodka did not agree with you? Please have a seat." Alexi waited several seconds before Luc acquired a seat beside him. "Yes, I also have sources my friend. Nothing is a secret in this country. I am the Premier am I not? And I have a good security chief who keeps me well informed," chiding Luc's duties as his KGB chief.

Alexi directed his attention to the unit in front of him. He withdrew a pair of well-worn reading glasses from his shirt pocket before closely inspecting the unit's details and diagrams.

He paused for a moment as he read the general outline of the unit's capabilities. When he reached the papers last line the documents suddenly slipped out of his hands—falling to the floor. Visibly shaken, he stood up, the potent vodka having lost its desired effect.

"This will upset the Americans to no avail, Comrade," Alexi said. "They could choose to launch a first strike if word leaks out of this weapons existence. That is what I would do if I were the American President. Are we willing to take the risk?"

Luc held his ground, nodding, "Yes, we should Comrade." He leaned forward to touch the case as he spoke, pushing it closer to his friend. "Think of it, Alexi,"— reverting to his friends given name instead of the less personal title he had been using up to that moment. "This one, bold, master stroke can put us back in the game. We could have the Americans by the proverbial balls. No longer will we have to back down from them as your predecessor did over Cuba. This is our chance, Comrade. It may be our last."

Luc removed a dagger from his jacket pocket, holding it up so Alexi could see the Nazi swastika emblazoned upon its wooden handle. It was the same dagger Luc had removed from a dead German officer during the battle for Stalingrad. Luc sliced his palm in one, swift stroke, handing the dagger across the table, motioning for Alexi to follow suit.

Alexi took the dagger, holding it in his right hand. The mere thought of the traitor Khrushchev made him cringe, his bottom lip curling up. He alone had allowed the Soviet Union to be humiliated before the world's stage as if it were some second rate nation bowing before its master. Upon Khrushchev's death, his name was struck from every Soviet history book. The mere mention of his name in conversation, private or public, meant an automatic 5-year sentence in a Siberian prison.

Alexi looked down at the dagger he held in his hands before slicing his own palm, then he reached for Luc's outstretched hand, ceremoniously intermingling their blood, and once again swearing an unspoken allegiance to mother Russia.

Alexi returned the ceremonial dagger to Luc, but not before wiping away the excess blood from its blade on his shirt. Neither spoke for the longest moment. Alexi's hand trembled as he poured himself a glass of water.

Realizing his friend was only trying to protect his country's honor, Alexi walked around the table to where Luc stood.

"Madman you may be, but allow this operation to proceed." He hugged his old friend before turning to leave. Pausing once more before he left the room, looking back at Luc, a smile breaking out on his face. "My friend, I feel as though we are back in this marathon we call a *Cold War*."

Luc resembled a young child on Christmas morning as he stood watching his friend depart for the night, enthusiastically banging on the conference table as if it were a child's drum set. He tried to contain his excitement as he snapped the suitcase back into place, hastily fastening a lead security breaker to seal the unit. Looking about the now empty room, he turned to face the door where the Premier had already departed.

"You are right my friend—*we are back in the marathon!*"

CHAPTER THREE

Present Day - Ocean City, New Jersey

A light breeze blew across the ocean waves as they broke effortlessly for the beach. A refreshing seawater mist evolved, one that would no doubt dampen all objects in its path. The narrow wooden bench that Peter Zarinsko occupied was no exception, facing the ocean that lay before him, basking in the late afternoon sun.

Of medium height, rail-thin with an olive-skinned complexion resembling someone of Italian descent. He blended in perfectly with the middle-aged yuppies that abounded.

Gazing from side-to-side, Peter wondered if it were all a dream. He had arrived in Philadelphia only three weeks ago. Once in Philadelphia, he had assumed the role of a typical tourist—following the script thoroughly detailed by his Syrian handlers during his training in Damascus.

As planned, he visited most of the usual historical sites located throughout the Delaware Valley; the Liberty Bell, Independence Hall, Valley Forge and the Betsy Ross House. He hoped to lull any agents of the US Government into a state of complacency. After September 11th, they suspected all people of his faith, he knew he would be followed—at least initially. Hopefully, after seeing his dull routine they would deem him as a simple "tourist" and leave him to fulfill his mission. Only then could he focus in on his primary targets.

With the mid-August temperature having breached the 95-degree mark, the beach that lay before him still had a respectable, yet dwindling population for the early evening hour. The remaining sun worshipers would soon roll up their cotton towels and heavy woolen beach blankets and trudge off to their expensive vacation rentals.

On the boardwalk behind him crowds thickened with toddlers manipulating parents from one amusement ride to another. Stuffing cotton candy in their mouths as they anxiously floated from ride-to-ride on a euphoria provided by the intoxicating combination of childish wonder and sugar. Not once did Peter notice a parent scold or reprimand his or her child for constantly wanting more. He was cautioned before leaving his homeland of Chechnya, and then once again during his training in Syria, that this kind of behavior was to be expected in the land of *milk and honey*.

From his prone position on the bench, he couldn't help but notice the scantily clad young women who plodded along the boardwalk. With his strict Islamic upbringing, Peter was initially shocked at such behavior but he gradually became accustomed to "the show" as the waning weeks of his mission flew by. He didn't mind this part of his work. This was all *"eye candy,"* another American slang term he had heard on more than one occasion but alas, something he would never see in his homeland.

Peter turned back towards the beach in time to see a dog as it leapt into the air to catch a Frisbee in its mouth. Peter admired the dog's skill for a few moments, waiting until the dog received a treat for his hard work. *Yes, when my work here is complete that dog will be similar to Russia, catching all that we throw, responding to our simplest demands.*

Peter Zarinsko had originally gone by his birth name, Muhammad Maizf, before assuming the new identity provided by his Syrian handlers for his mission to the United States.

He was born in the state of Chechnya to an uneducated tailor and a housekeeper; the oldest of eight brothers and sisters. At the age of 15, Peter's father recognized the boy's leadership qualities and pushed the young boy to apply to the Frunze Military Academy, Russia's equivalent of the American West Point. His father hoped Peter would someday become a military officer and escape the cycle of living in squalor.

Once accepted, Peter did not disappoint. He thrived in the Frunze's esteemed traditions and camaraderie. Through hard work and dedication, he graduated at the top of his class and earned an assignment to Chechnya as his reward.

Once back in his homeland, he rapidly rose through the ranks, eventually assuming command of Chechnya's only military armory in Grozny. When Chechnya declared its independence from Russia, it was Peter's job to defend the armory until the reserve Russian Army units could arrive in force from their bases located on the outskirts of the city. It would be their job to remove the inventory of weapons for safekeeping. Though he was a Russian officer, his inner allegiance lay with his home state of Chechnya. Instead of fighting his fellow compatriots in its bid for independence, Peter instructed his troops to lay down their weapons and surrender to the mobs that soon gathered around the last bastion of Russia sovereignty in their city. Peter tossed open the doors of the armory to the masses, distributing its weapons and ammunition to aid its citizens in their fight for independence. Soon after, he fled to the hills and mountains of Chechnya, now charged with killing Russian soldiers instead of leading them.

He had to evict them from *his* country, for *they* were now the enemy.

Now, after twenty long years of civil war, the battles that had ravaged his country were about to end, victorious for his country if he could follow through with his mission in the United States. The rebel leadership had already appointed Peter as the next martyr for their country.

Unfortunately for him, to attain martyr status—*he would have to die.*

Peter rested heavily on the bench, wondering if his Russian contact would ultimately show up for their meeting. *He did say 8 pm in the last E-mail message? Not 8 am?* Nervously fidgeting as he scanned the immediate area for any sign of his comrade.

Before arriving in the United States, Peter had been provided with a list of Public Libraries in the Philadelphia area where he would receive further instructions. He simply accessed an Arabic web page run by Syrian intelligence, looking for a message posted under Muhammad Maizf for further instructions. Once he opened his message, it would provide a number from one to 10, a meeting time and an identifying object to wear. The first number was to be associated with a location. So for a typical meeting, the message was broken out as: 3, 8 pm, Beach Boys, 8/17. The number three stood for; Ocean City Boardwalk, Mack & Mancos pizza, bench against beach. Then the time: 8pm, then what type of shirt to wear for recognition and finally the date. The code was simplistic in its composition, yet unbreakable. The instructions and meeting times meant nothing to anyone reading them, unless you had the exact locations associated with the times. And these were only provided to Peter before he had left Syria, which he promptly memorized and ripped into pieces before disposing of them in the aircraft lavatory.

The Ocean City Boardwalk made for easy meet location due to the masses of people that typically gathered on a Saturday evening. The more people, the easier to mingle in and get lost once the exchange was complete.

Boris Stevensky enjoyed living the good life since his retirement. Unfortunately, retirement had also added many pounds to his small stature, providing him with a Buddha-like girth. His shaven head only enhanced the look. His Swiss doctors pleaded with him to shed some of the weigh. He ignored them all, referring to them as "witch-doctors."

At one time Boris was considered the top KGB agent for the old Soviet Union. Now, under the new Russian auspices, the KGB was better known as the Federal Security Service or FSB. He was "old school" KGB, having trained most of the FSB leadership now in place, knowing exactly where their criminal mindset and reputations lay.

His rise to the top was derailed when caught in a compromising situation with a female FBI agent. At the time, he was employed as one of the Soviet Union's Senior Cultural Liaison's at its Washington Embassy, working directly for the KGB Station Chief. It was the old "honey pot" in reverse, with many American diplomats having been caught in the same embarrassing situation. His expulsion from the country effectively ended his overseas career. Upon his return home, his superiors assigned him to a minor position at the KGB training academy in Volgograd. In effect, hoping Boris would just simply fade away. But Boris had an ace up his sleeve: his photographic memory. He could view a document for only a few seconds and commit the document to memory.

As one of the lead "spooks" at the Soviet Union's Washington DC embassy, he experienced many an opportunity to view "red" or "for your eyes only" documents meant for the Ambassador or KGB Station Chief. On one such occasion he was able to view an extraordinary document, one titled *The Devil's Suitcase*, and would never leave the recesses of his mind. He knew the document would have immense value at some point in his future.

Boris despised what Russia had become in its downward spiral from its super power status only years before. Now she lay regulated to hovering between a second or third-rate nation. He had visions that possibly with a little push from his end, the real Russia could once again emerge and regain to its rightful position of power.

Boris had provided Peter with instructions to stand in front of the bench as a signal if being monitored or tailed, this way Boris would simply walk by unnoticed. His years of undercover experience taught him never to relax. The one time you did, you would be caught. *Just like his honey pot sting.*

Boris cursed silently as he exited the air-conditioned shop. He had never become accustomed to weather in the states, even after spending six long years in Washington DC.

In front of him the boardwalks pedestrian traffic maintained some resemblance of an American highway with both the right and left hand side's moving according to roadway etiquette. He waited for a break in the flow before merging and walking toward the ocean side of the boardwalk. He continually scanned the crowd for anyone that may stand out from the ordinary tourist.

After 30 years of being in *the business*, Boris could detect someone who seemed out of place. Anyone sporting a "high and tight" haircut was usually the easiest to spot, this being the preferred cut for most law enforcement types. Suit and ties were a dead giveaway—inexpensive ones at that. Policing agencies in the United States were not known for being generous when it came to dealing with their clothing allowance. Such a shame thought Boris, scanning the crowd for any tell tale signs. The United States could learn a lesson or two from the Russian FSB. Maybe on his next trip to the US he could make a pitch to one of his old advisories in the

FBI, maybe even teach a class on how criminals evade police surveillance.

Sweating profusely as he walked the remaining distance to his contact, Boris knew this would be the make or break point; the final few meters. *Should he just walk past and drop the envelope near his contacts feet?* Such a move would allow him to blend safely into the background and keep pace with the jostling crowd. *No, he could not take the chance of the envelope falling through the board's cracks and to the beach below. This would not be prudent with several billion dollar's worth of state-owned product on hand!*

Ever vigilant, he looked from side-to-side as he stopped to mop his brow. Satisfied the area was indeed clear—he sat down heavily beside his contact.

Initially caught off guard, Peter dropped his slice of his pizza on his pants before it slipped to the boardwalk.

Boris tried to conceal a slight smile not wanting to offend his young Muslim contact realizing it was probably his first undercover operation.

Boris reached underneath his Panama Jack shirt and pulled out a white manila business envelope. He delicately wrapped it with a handkerchief, handing it to Peter as if to assist with the spill.

Peter realized what Boris was trying to do and willingly accepted the handkerchief, thanking the polite stranger that he was.

Using the handkerchief to blot the red pizza sauce off his pants, Peter slipped the envelope between his legs.

Boris glanced at Peter out of the corner of his eye, careful to keep his head aligned straight as if looking towards the beach. He sat there silently wondering if this young man were as brave and idealistic as his Syrian handlers stated he would be. The information Boris had received on his subject was clear; graduated at the top of his class, he excelled at every opportunity provided. But Boris wondered if he could follow through on an operation he himself had lost the nerve to perform several years before. He personally had no stomach for it. Age does that to a man.

Within three days, the whole world would know if his Syrian handlers were accurate.

The simple exchange of the business envelope complete, Boris calmly bent down as if to tie his shoes. "We are off the communication cycle. No more meetings, phone calls or e-mails." He now worked on the other lace. "I am disappearing after this. I do not expect to be connected with this operation in any way. Do you understand what I am saying my young friend? I am a ghost."

"Yes, all according to your plan, sir," Peter responded in near flawless English, a product of his Frunze Military Academy training. "I have everything we will need right here," patting the envelope Boris had delivered to him. "You can now retreat back to your safe house knowing you have performed a great deed with your actions here today. Allah and my country will be eternally grateful for your divine intervention."   •

Boris pondered Peter's response for a moment. Why did he make it a point to say *safe house*? What else did the Syrians tell this man?

Boris turned to face the young man for the first time since sitting down. "You're right to assume I have a safe house. I maintain a small villa in Switzerland. It's my insurance policy where I hope to live out my remaining days."

Peter carefully picked up his pizza slice from the boardwalk, tossing it onto the beach near an unsuspecting pack of seagulls. He watched as the seagulls attacked the food in earnest, then each other, for the edible prize.

"There will be nothing to connect you with the events of the next three days. You have *my word* on that. My people are grateful for all you have done. We would never allow any harm to come to our friends. The only people you should fear are the infidels you associate with. They are the ones who will turn on you like Jackal's—*not my fellow brothers.*"

Boris stepped over to the rail that separated the beach from the boardwalk, still confident he was within earshot of Peter. "In my youth, I studied the great Roman and Greek empires. I was fascinated with their histories, philosophies, and the teachings they provided. One particular area of interest was myths, both of the Roman and Greek variety." He paused for several seconds, looking back to see if he still held his Muslim friend's attention.

Peter nodded for him to proceed.

"Well here I am spouting off about something that may or may not interest you but here goes. The ancient Romans had a myth about the sea. A beautiful sea-maiden sits on a rock, blowing kisses to all sailors who happen by, trying to lure them into her domain. Of course, her beauty is so enticing they choose to sail closer. The closer they sail, the more her beauty becomes apparent. It's at this point the vision suddenly disappears, changing back to reality; a rock. This happens all too late for the poor misguided sailors, for they collide with the rock and are tossed into the sea. The sea maiden then dutifully rises up to swallow the results of her actions."

He paused for several seconds allowing the words true meaning to sink in before continuing. "Well, with that envelope you now have in your possession, I hope you are not a sailor with a vision of a sea-maiden. May God or Allah or whomever you choose to worship have mercy on your soul." Boris turned quickly and disappeared into the crowd.

Peter slipped the envelope into his pants pocket. He faced in the direction of what he hoped was east, closing his eyes for a few moments of silent prayer. When finished, he stood and made his way through the crowd in order to buy another slice of pizza before his long journey.

As he waited for his order, Peter viewed the pageantry that was still in progress on the boardwalk. His eyes followed the progress of a bevy of young women who were parading past him. Cheap knock-offs of Channel and Gucci hung the night air competing with the aroma of his pizza cooking.

Both possessed their own intoxicating qualities.

A smile creased his face as he looked to his left, this time noticing a man with an earpiece and military style haircut quickly look away, now peering into a shop window that sold women's bathing suits. Peter's natural instincts seized control.

The man had to be either a pervert or a cop. Peter settled on cop.

The man's combination of long pants and loose, baggy shirt, made it easy to conceal any weapon he may have tucked into his waistband. Now the million-dollar question—was he local or Fed? If local, it shouldn't be a problem. He might just be working on a shoplifting detail and Peter could have looked suspicious with his Arabic profile. If he is a Fed—*well, that would be a problem.*

Peter realized he couldn't run. No, it had to be the bathroom or nothing. He walked to the back of the small, crowded shop, maneuvering around a pile of empty cardboard pizza boxes neatly stacked from floor-to-ceiling. Once in the bathroom, he hastily bolted the door behind him. With only one escape route before him, he climbed on top of toilet's ceramic water tank and after some minor effort, was able to push open the bathroom's only window.

Peter peered out the windows narrow opening only to view a trash-laden alley below. Looking from side-to-side, he noticed another man walking towards him—only this gentleman wore a cheaply cut suit. Peter braced himself against the wall to avoid falling, collecting his thoughts as his mind raced.

"Damn it," he said aloud, closing the window.

He paused for a few seconds on his water tank perch, mentally retracing his earlier drive from Philadelphia, coming to the conclusion that it must have been the Russian who slipped up. Peter knew he was cornered and would have no choice but to fight his way out.

Peter made his way back to the front counter. Better to play along. The agent was easy enough to notice, him leaning against the shops wall enjoying his own slice of pizza. Peter smiled, having heard that most police in the United States only hung around donut shops or all-night convenience stores. *This must be a real treat for him.*

Peter eased a five-dollar bill across the counter to pay for his slice of pizza.

Then he felt a light tap on his arm.

Not bothering to turn, he chose to ignore the agent who now stood alongside the counter. Peter needed additional time to figure a way out.

As the seconds passed he once again felt a tap on his arm, this one more pronounced. Realizing he couldn't ignore the agent any longer, he responded by turning and coming face-to-face with the man.

He flashed an FBI badge, motioning for him to walk outside.

Peter knew the agent was operating alone due to his partner still being in the rear alley. He had to move quickly and overpower his enemy before the other agent showed up.

Looking for anything that might be utilized as a weapon, Peter settled on the only object within his reach—slamming his steaming hot slice of pizza into the agents face.

The ensuing confusion allowed Peter to rush out the door before the agent could react, disappearing into the ever-thickening Saturday night crowd.

The agent fell to his knees in agony as the pizza's hot cheese and sauce scalded his face. His cries of pain were overheard by his partner via the radio link he carried in his pocket.

His partner bolted from his alley position arriving in time to see Peter escaping through the crowd almost 50 yards away.

The agent from the alley paused briefly as he checked on his partner's status—his partner on his knees with his badge and weapon lying sprawled in front of him.

Satisfied his partner had only superficial wounds, he bolted down the boardwalk in pursuit of his suspect.

Peter was able to put some distance between the pizza shop and the agent — before pausing to look back and see another agent in dogged pursuit. He realized he had to pick up his pace knowing the agent would no doubt be calling in local support.

The thickening crowd slowed Peter. He knew the slow pace would only increase his chances of capture. To his right, he noticed a children's arcade. Looking back, he lost site of the agent who was in pursuit. He had only one option. Peter bolted into the arcade. Once inside he immediately sought out the manager—easily identifiable by the change dispenser he sported about his thick waist.

Peter pulled a fifty-dollar bill from his pocket before thrusting it in the man's face. "I'm playing a game with my children. I have a Type A personality and just have to win, I can't let them find me," Peter said, slightly out of breath. "I have to use your alley exit."

Little Jimmy Salvino, all 6 foot 4, 350 pounds of him, inherited the arcade from his father, *Big Jim*, 10 years earlier. He had to admit that this was a first—someone paying $50 bucks to use a door. Thinking about his alimony payment coming due in the ensuing week he readily agreed. "No problem. You go straight back and through the office. It will lead you to the alley." He quickly snatched the fifty from Peter's hand before he had a chance to reconsider.

Less than 30 seconds elapsed before an FBI agent and three Ocean City Police officers converged from opposite directions, meeting conveniently outside "Little Jimmy's" arcade.

"Where the hell did he go?" the pursuing FBI Agent shouted to the local police officers, both with their weapons drawn, hungrily looking for any reason to discharge them for the first time in their careers. "I was chasing him towards you. He couldn't just disappear!"

Little Jimmy noticed the commotion outside his arcade and went to investigate. *They were scaring away his potential customers.* "What's up with guns drawn like the Wild West?" he said to no one in particular.

The officer closest to him responded first. "We have a suspect loose around here and can't seem to find where the son of a bitch went."

It didn't take long for Little Jimmy to realize who they were looking for. "Hey wait a minute. Some bum just used my alley door. He said he was playing a game with his kids and had to find an exit real quick. The guy had a dark complexion, skinny. He looked like an Arab."

"That's our man," the FBI agent said, rudely brushing past Little Jimmy in search of the arcade's alley door. "He's moving towards his car."

Peter had enough foresight to park his car in one of the various pay lots adjacent to the boardwalk's many on/off ramps. He was already gunning his engine by the time the FBI agent turned the corner with his local police contingent in tow—a mere 50 yards away.

The Agent leveled his weapon to fire at Peter's car but, at the last minute, wisely held back due to the crowd of bystanders on the busy street.

Peter wasted no time, his tires squealed as he quickly sped off. With his cover blown, he had no choice but to proceed with his backup plan.

Satisfied he had outrun his pursers, Peter steered his car to the main route moving south. No doubt the FBI and police would set up roadblocks going north towards Philadelphia. He had to outsmart them. *Going in the direction they least expected.*

Peter still had another hour until he reached his alternate site. As he drove, he focused on the list the former KGB agent had provided him. According to his Syrian trainers the KGB list would include the exact location of two, suitcase sized, nuclear warheads. The Syrians said the Soviets buried the weapons in the United States during the late 1970's as "insurance" to hold off the United States and still maintain its deadly threat—a subtle one, but one ever so present. For this "insurance," the Soviet Union chose to smuggle thirty-four, "suitcase" sized warheads into the US via diplomatic shipments.

Using this cover, the Soviet Union shipped the 40 pound, 3-foot by 2-foot by 2-foot thick black lead-lined cases to the US with routine cargo traveling to the Soviet Union's Embassy in Washington DC during the 1976-79 timeframe. Upon their arrival in the United States, each suitcase was dispersed to a predetermined location personally chosen by the Soviet Premier and the KGB Directorate Chief.

Once all the warheads were all dispersed, the Soviet Union's KGB Washington office purposely leaked information about their existence to the American CIA. At first, the Americans brushed it aside as another KGB hoax. The Soviets then offered one of the weapons as a "sacrificial lamb" for the Americans. What had they to lose? Once a deal was brokered between the two agencies, a lone CIA agent accompanied one KGB Agent to suitcase number seventeen's location. Number seventeen lay buried on the grounds of the Washington DC Headquarters of the Treasury Building, 2-1/2 feet below a row of Abraham Lincoln rose bushes on the eastern side of the building—*and a mere 1 block from the White House*. When the suitcase weapon was retrieved from its earthen grave, the CIA weapons expert was horrified, instantly realizing this was no hoax.

The expert recognized the weapon was of such sophistication it would have instantly wiped out everyone and everything with-in an 8-block radius of detonation; eventually killing many more through radiation poisoning that would linger for weeks after the initial explosion.

The 8-block area they presently stood in included: the White House, Capitol Building, FBI Headquarters, Treasury Building, and the Supreme Court.

The CIA expert reportedly blessed himself and said a silent prayer as the KGB Agent verified the weapons status.

Once removed from its concealed location, the KGB Agent carefully re-packaged the weapon for shipment and escort back to its Washington Embassy—all as agreed before hand with the CIA.

The Soviets were not about to turn over one of their most potent and complex weapons for dissection to an adversary such as the American CIA. This was just a game of show and tell. The Soviets had revealed their hand, now it was time for the Americans to run off like Paul Revere.

After the information and the initial shock wore off, the CIA realized the Soviet Union's vast spy network located within the United States was considered even more potent and dangerous then its master. The possibility even existed that a small cadre of undercover personnel could strike the US even if the Soviet Union were to become incapacitated during a first strike scenario. Even more troublesome to the boys at Langley was the realization that the Soviets also had the ability to perform its own first strike on US facilities. Under this scenario, the United States Command structure at NORAD would have no warning of the actual strike until it was already over. This meant it would already be too late for a response since the Soviets would have wisely planted the weapons near the only persons and facilities authorized to strike back.

For a generation the US military planned for a massive nuclear response if its command at NORAD-Cheyenne Mountain detected a weapons launch. Now the rules of engagement had suddenly changed.

How could they respond to a weapons detonation, on its own soil, without proof of responsibility?

If the US held any advantage up to this point, this effectively evened the playing field or even tilted it slightly in the Soviets favor. As the CIA would discover years latter via their own Russian spy network, the weapons were ultimately buried near major military and high profile civilian installations. Included on the short list was a location in Langley, Virginia—a mere four blocks from CIA headquarters.

The Russian Government reportedly kept the "need to know" list short. Only nine of its citizens knew the exact locations of the buried weapons. What the Russian Government overlooked was the possibility of the list having been compromised by someone else—possibly a trained spy who also spied on their own people when it suited their own interests. With this type of person included, the list reached a total of 10 or 11 who possessed the Godlike knowledge.

Boris infiltrated or "examined" his boss's office on a periodic basis to keep abreast of situations that had or might arise, always wanting to stay ahead.

On one such occasion, the list of suitcase weapons locations presented themselves by making an appearance on his boss's desk, right in the open for all to see. Boris simply copied the list in shorthand, and then memorized the locations over the next several days and nights. This allowed Boris to burn any evidence of the list and keep this one piece of information as his potential trump card for years to come, waiting until the time was right to shrewdly make his move.

This was just such a time—but he would only lay down two of his aces—keeping the remaining 32 for some future actions should the need arise.

The person in receipt of those "aces" was one, Peter Zarinsko, thanks to the actions of Boris Stevensky.

The short list who knew of the existence of the suitcase weapons had now grown by a one, making Chechnya *the world's newest nuclear power and the eighth most powerful county in the world.*

CHAPTER FOUR

Present day; Southern Chechnya

The early morning snowstorm boded well for Captain Igor Isinov as he concealed himself in his pine branch lean-to, fingering his TAC-nine automatic weapon. With a lean, muscular body supporting his 6-foot tall frame, he could physically endure anything Mother Nature tossed his way.

He expected no less of his troops.

The snow had completely masked any previous trace of his unit's activities. The calendar still showed August but the mountains of Chechnya lay coated with snow as if Austria in December. The freak snowstorm was unusual for the time of year with the first storms usually arriving in September.

Captain Isinov and his five-man KARKOV (Special Forces Anti-Terrorism and Assault Volunteers) unit parachuted out of a Russian Air Force aircraft deep into Chechen territory the previous night. They were searching for signs of the Rebel Mujahedeen Army headquarters rumored to be operating in the area. For them, the snow was a blessing; it would enable them to track their prey by simply following their footprints in the snow.

Captain Isinov did not mind the bone chilling cold, nor the snow, just happy to be "in the game" as his team referred to it. After 17 years of Russian Army miscues, the Russian High Command had decided to seek out a "full effort" on ending the war in Chechnya.

First formed in 1979 as an elite, first strike, anti-terrorism weapon, KARKOV was comprised of volunteers from across the Russian Special Forces. It was a knee-jerk reaction to the American Military forming DELTA units to combat anti-terrorism. "If it's good enough for the Americans—*it was a necessity for the Russians*," was a common joke in the KARKOV community.

KARKOV achieved its legendary status in the counter-terrorism world with its dramatic rescue of 65 Aeroflot passengers in 1994 from militant Islamic terrorists in Azerbaijan. With the Russian jet parked on the Tarmac and ten, armed to the teeth terrorists on board, KARKOV troops stormed the jet with 20 of its own troops. Within the ensuing two minutes, all ten terrorists lay dead from clean shots to the head.

For seven years Captain Isinov and his fellow KARKOV members pressured the Russian Duma to release them for service in Chechnya. Under mounting pressure due to heavy losses, the Russian government finally relented and allowed them into combat.

With KARKOV being in a position to act independently of the main forces, this enabled them to undertake missions that they alone planned, not to be used as fodder or replacement troops.

As KARKOV's reputation grew due to its military actions in Chechnya, they eventually received carte blanche to undertake any mission, anytime, anywhere. The government-sponsored newspapers began touting KARKOV's military prowess; writing lengthy articles on their exploits as they tried to single handedly save the reputation of the Russian Army in Chechnya.

After receiving much fanfare in Moscow, even the Russian President followed KARKOV's daily exploits in dispatches and reports from his on-site Commanders. With this type of notoriety, no Russian Field Commander would dare turn down a KARKOV request for support unless he was prepared to explain his justification to the Russian President himself.

Captain Isinov's men placed a three-sided box grid of 15 anti-personnel mines before the snow had fallen, placing two groups of five mines in straight lines on both sides of the path and an additional five in front of the "box." This allowed an unsuspecting group to walk in but provided no clear exit.

The mines were of the new sensor class. When contact with the first mine was established, they would all explode in unison, decimating an entire platoon if the mines were positioned correctly.

Captain Isinov directed two of his men to position themselves on opposite sides of the trail. He then placed the remaining two in the rear to effectively "close the box," providing a classic, textbook ambush. From previous information, the footpath in front of them operated as the main "road" between the rebel front and their Mujahedeen Headquarters in the rear.

From his vantage point, Captain Isinov had a difficult time viewing his men as they burrowed themselves into the natural environment with the snow providing additional ground cover for their positions. A sense of pride overcame him.

The rebel units contained some of the best mountain fighters he had ever come to know. They could infiltrate an unsuspecting unit's defenses in a matter of minutes, killing most, if not all, before quickly, *melting away*. Of course, it could never happen to a KARKOV unit.

In the latest incident, KARKOV troops were able to pick up the trail and hunt down the rebel unit associated with several of the atrocities. Catching them less than 15 kilometers from the previous incident, killing them in the same manner in which they had doled out to the Russian forces. The men even decapitated some of the rebel victims for mounting on sticks and poles, placing them around the overrun rebel camp for their comrades to view.

Due to their success, the Russian High Command selected KARKOV troops to seek out the location of the rebel headquarters. They hoped KARKOV could pinpoint the location for a massive strike by the Russian Air Force.

Previous Special Forces attempts had failed to achieve any note of satisfaction with the High Command, with most units slaughtered or forced to retreat. The actions also cost the Russian military many specialized troops and a bounty of equipment that the rebels quickly turned against the occupying Russian troops.

The Russian Special Forces were excellent fighters on open terrain where the enemy could not find suitable cover. When it came to fighting in the mountainous terrain south of Grozny, they were utterly inept in comparison to the rebel forces. These high-profile failures led the Russian Army Command to finally buckle and open the door for KARKOV participation.

After five hours of patiently waiting for their bounty, they were rewarded with what appeared to be a column of rebels moving silently along the trail and heading directly for their "box." Upon viewing the distant figures slowly approach his troop's position, Captain Isinov silently released the safety from his TAC-nine. He watched as the rebels walked single-file in a haphazard fashion no more than 20 meters from where his men patiently waited. He counted 11, each bundled against the piercing cold in layers of colorfully assorted clothing, resembling a moving circus train, all topped with traditional head garb.

The rebel group leader had placed three men in front of the column, and two in the rear, all heavily armed as they wearily eyed the surrounding woods. The remaining six walked in the middle of the column with their weapons slung over their shoulders, carrying boxes of ammunition on solid wood poles, each strung between them in groups of two, each box resembling a pig on a split.

They walked unwittingly into the ambush on a trail they had probably walked numerous times before. Suddenly one of them stepped onto the first contact mine that lay in his path. The force of the resulting explosion lifted the now legless body five feet into the air, dropping him back down with a dull thud. The ensuing explosion turned bone fragments from the man's legs into shrapnel, slicing through the soldier following him, killing him instantly.

The first explosion then triggered the remaining 14 mines to detonate on both sides of the column, sending jagged pieces of hot metal in all directions around them, killing two outright and wounding the remainder.

Captain Isinov and his troops took advantage of the confusion, firing short bursts from their concealed positions, eliminating six more of the rebels before they even had a chance to use their weapons.

The last rebel in the rear of the column dove behind a cluster of rocks that shielded him from his attacker's bullets.

It would have been easy for Captain Isinov to toss a grenade into the rock cluster and be on their way, but this was the prisoner they sought. The rebel must be taken alive. *In order to have an interrogation—they required someone who could still talk.*

Sirna Muliruid realized the desperate position he was in, firing bursts from his concealed position, hoping to keep his attackers at bay until Allah could provide some assistance. If he could hold them off for a few minutes, maybe they would vanish just as quickly as they appeared. The shooting and explosions might possibly attract some of his fellow Mujahedeen soldiers from their positions north of here. He wiped blood from his weathered face, evidently a piece of shrapnel had found its mark above his untrimmed beard. All he could do was hope and pray as he reloaded his AK-47 with the last of his ammunition. *What an irony, enough ammunition to hold off an army was only meters away and here I am with nothing left to fight with.*

How could it end here? He thought to himself. *I have survived numerous missions against the Russian devils, escaping each time to fight another day.* Sirna Miliruid was not about to die lying in a hole, not like some animal giving birth. If he were going to die, it would like a man, charging the devils in his quest to reach Allah.

Yes, Allah would welcome him with a huge feast.

Slowly he counted to three.

Captain Isinov ordered his men to stay concealed. He alone would approach the remaining fighter. Cautiously, he approached within grenade distance, a mere 10 meters from the rebel fighter's position. He secretly admired the man for not immediately surrendering, also for locating the only defensible position in the immediate area.

Captain Isinov once again motioned for his troops to stay in their positions, still unsure if the rebel had any stragglers lurking behind him somewhere in the woods. Pulling a stun grenade from his web belt, he counted to three before tossing it into the rebel's rock stronghold.

Sirna Miliruid rose up from his position, his AK-47 blazing away before a brilliant flash temporarily blinded him along with its accompanying explosion, his eardrums bursting in the same instant. The combination of both dropped him to his knees in searing pain as he wondered aloud if he were dead or alive, crying out to Allah for guidance.

Captain Isinov saw his victim incapacitated for the moment; he rushed the remaining ten meters to the rebels' position, diving over the outcrop of rock and landing on top of Sirna. He wrestled with Sirna to place plastic handcuffs about his wrists, amazed at the physical strength the man still displayed after the paralyzing blow of the stun grenade.

The captain's fellow troops arrived in time to assist placing the cuffs on Sirna, helping to flip him over onto back, face-up.

Seeing the situation now under control, Captain Isinov efficiently deployed two of his troops 50 meters in opposite directions. He then ordered the remaining men to search the dead rebels for anything that might be of importance.

Turning back to face his new prisoner, Captain Isinov removed a pack of American cigarettes from his pocket. He cupped his hands as he carefully lit the cigarette against the bitter wind that blew in from the west. He took his time inhaling before leaning down to blow smoke on his young captives face.

Sirna stared back defiantly.

"Where were you going, comrade?" Captain Isinov said in a tone meant more for scolding a young child, not a seasoned warrior such as Sirna. "Were you walking to, or from your headquarters?" Pointing up the trail, then he motioned behind him.

Sirna Miliruid spit at Isinov's fur boots, missing them by mere inches.

Captain Isinov looked down at the near miss and smiled as he took another long drag on the cigarette, holding the smoke in his mouth for a few seconds before again exhaling directly into Sirna's face.

Sirna coughed in response.

Captain Isinov was well aware that devout Muslims refrained from smoking, a filthy vice he had picked up as a mercenary fighting in Angola many years before. He puffed rapidly on the cigarette, effectively allowing the ash on its edge to become as hot as possible before plunging the cigarette directly into Sirna's forehead, directly above his right eye.

Sirna winced from the pain but did not struggle or turn away.

Captain Isinov was just warming up as he lifted his boot and brutally smashed it against Sirna's face, breaking his nose in two places, allowing blood to flow freely down his lips and chin before finally dripping down to the crisp white snow beneath him.

Sirna realized he was facing a long, painful death at the hands of this infidel, but in the end, he would be rewarded with Allah and his friends. He silently prayed as Captain Isinov brutally pulled him up to a standing position before striking him in his abdomen, causing him to double over in pain from the blow.

Captain Isinov brutally shoved Sirna to the ground where his head struck a rock, knocking off his traditional head garb.

"Tell me the location of your headquarters complex, and I will allow you a quick and merciful death," Captain Isinov demanded. He now walked around Sirna, acting as if he were an animal circling his prey, preparing for a second strike. "You have my word as a Russian officer."

Sirna strained to stand up, resembling a young colt struggling for its balance. Once up, he moved to within a meter of Captain Isinov's face.

"God is Great, Allah Akbar," Sirna shouted, spitting blood on the Russians white, winter parka.

Captain Isinov shook his head in disbelief, taking a drag from his cigarette before forcefully shoving him back down to the ground. "I am trying to be as kind as possible. You are pushing me to my limits." He pulled a ½ liter of vodka from the inside lining of his parka. "Can you please tell me the location of your headquarters?" he said, his eyes never leaving Sirna's. He raised the bottle to his lips to take a small sip before pouring the remaining contents of the bottle on Sirna's outer clothing. He smiled as he then removed a lighter from his pocket.

Sirna knew what was coming next, closing his eyes in silent prayer.

"Captain, Captain Isinov," came a cry from Corporal Tupol. "I think we have another live one."

Captain Isinov placed his lighter back into his pocket, pointing at his prisoner in the same instant. "You have a temporary stay of execution. Enjoy the time while you can." He turned to a soldier evaluating captured documents. "Private Krimiv come over here and stand guard over this man. If he so much as twitches, you have my permission to smash his face in. But don't kill him," leaning down to Sirna. "He's mine."

Captain Isinov strode to where Corporal Tupol stood over a mangled, legless body, careful not to slip in the blood trail that flowed in both directions. "What is it Corporal? What is so important that you drag me away from my interrogation?" Captain Isinov looked down in pity at the rebel, clearly in delirium from the combination of shock with the loss of his legs.

"He keeps mumbling something about his brother and the end of the war will soon be coming," the Corporal said, kicking the body to have him repeat the words. "Say it again comrade before you pass on to your God. Tell me more about the end of the war. What do you know?"

Rufa Miliruid lay in a state of delirium, passing in and out of consciousness as he lay in the fresh bed of snow looking up at the two figures clad in white standing over him. *Maybe the Christians are right, angels do exist!* Thinking for a moment he must be dead, for he felt no pain.

Rufa suddenly screamed deliriously: "Find my brother; he is the Commander of our unit! I need to say goodbye to him one last time. He has to fulfill the mission for us. We must end the war victorious."

Captain Isinov looked over to where he had left his prisoner in the hands of Private Krimiv, signaling for him to come over. "Private, bring the prisoner over here with you and hurry; we don't have much time."

Captain Isinov removed his field pack, unclipping his medical kit, extracting a needle containing morphine. He tapped it a few times with his forefinger shooting a small dose into the air before jabbing it into the rebels arm. He hoped the morphine would extend the man's life long enough to obtain additional information. *The morphine might also loosen his tongue.*

After several seconds, a sense of relief surged over Rufa, his eyelids fluttering several times.

"Get over here and tell me who this man is!" demanded Captain Isinov to Sirna, tossing him harshly down beside Rufa. "He is in your unit. Now tell me who the hell he is!" He pushed Sirna's head to within inches of Rufa Miliruid's face. "Do you recognize this man?"

"I do not know him," Sirna said unconvincingly. "He was placed in my unit at the last moment."

Captain Isinov brutally pulled Sirna's hair back, almost breaking his neck in the process. "You are a lying little pig. You answered too readily." He tossed him to one side leaning down over the legless Rufa. "Can you hear me comrade?"

Rufa nodded.

"Good. I have provided you with some medicine to ease your pain comrade. Now, I have some questions for you."

Rufa opened his eyes, surprised to see his brother at his feet, reaching out to him with his still functioning right hand.

Captain Isinov couldn't help but notice the sign of recognition.

"Do you know this man my friend?" Captain Isinov inquired, leaning down to comfort Rufa, lifting his head gently and pointing to Sirna.

"Sirna Miliruid, my brother, our great field commander." He tried to touch him before surrendering to the convulsions that raked his body.

Captain Isinov laid Rufa's head gently down in the snow, whispering for him to rest for his time with his God would soon be forthcoming.

Captain Isinov turned to Sirna. "As a humanitarian gesture I will provide you with a few seconds to say good-bye to your brave brother. Sorry, I must apologize but we can't leave you two alone; it wouldn't be prudent now would it?"

Looking at Sirna for some type of response, sensing none, he continued. "I take it that you choose not to participate in my gesture of good will?"

Sirna's head remained bowed.

"Private Krimiv, I am losing my touch. I am becoming too soft in my old age," said Captain Isinov jokingly, removing his weapon from his holster and placing it inches from Rufa's left ear. "Are you sure you have nothing to say to your brother? Not many people would get this second chance?"

Again with no response from Sirna, Captain Isinov casually pulled the trigger ending Rufa's life with a single bullet to his head.

"I can be generous and show compassion when it is warranted." He re-holstered his weapon, smiling at Sirna. "It is Sirna Miliruid, is it not? A dying man would not lie to us would he? No, I don't think so. Now if I remember correctly, Sirna Miliruid is the Field Commander for the Rebel Eastern sector."

Sirna did not flinch, knowing his brother had already been taken by Allah's hand.

"Corporal, signal our air team to be at the extraction point in two hours. Also inform them we will need immediate transport to Moscow after landing in Grozny."

Sirna knew he had to escape or kill himself before they evacuated him to Moscow. If they brought him to Moscow alive, he could surely betray his comrade's plans. He knew the Russians used drugs and torture to assist in the interrogation process, making it impossible to hold back any information. Sirna and his compatriots had much to lose if he lived, including the principle operation in the United States.

The captain mockingly saluted Sirna before he turned to walk away.

The corporal laughed aloud as leaned over to feel the pulse of the prisoner.

Sirna saw the opportunity Allah had presented to him. He sprung up from his kneeling position as if a coiled cobra lunging at its prey, slamming his body heavily into the corporal, applying a sharp head butt to his exposed fore head, knocking the corporal unconscious atop his brother.

Captain Isinov turned in time to view Sirna sprawled overtop of the corporal.

Sirna desperately clawed with his cuffed hands at the corporal's belt. "I will avenge your death, my brother," he said aloud as he pulled a grenade out of the belts webbing, struggling in vain to reach the metal release pin.

Fingering the grenade, he rotated it until he felt the metal hoop that signaled the pin. A smile broke across his face knowing his plan would succeed.

As he struggled to pull the pin, a sharp blow rendered him unconscious.

CHAPTER FIVE

Ocean City, New Jersey

Boris Stevensky mopped the perspiration from his brow as he left Peter sitting alone on the bench by the beach, trying to fade unnoticed into the boardwalk crowd. Boris smugly realized that he had just dropped off an envelope with a black market worth of between $2 - 4 Billion US dollars. But that price reflected just how badly a country desired the information and how much money they were willing to pay to become a nuclear nation.

The absurdity of it all triggered a smile to suddenly appear. Everyone could always use a few extra dollars, especially an extra *billion or two*. Not that the thought had not crossed his mind. He wasn't a greedy man, satisfied with the monies he had secreted in his Antigua and Swiss bank accounts.

As the former second in command of the Embassies KGB unit, Boris had access to a bank account the Soviet Union had used to subsidize its US spy network. The bank account at any one time contained close to $25 Million American dollars. With Boris being one of only four people who had access to the account, he had the ability to manipulate the figures paid out to his network of spy's, and at the same time, skim some cream from the top.

Over the first part of his career, Boris never so much as took a single ruble or payout from anyone, choosing the straight and narrow course. But as he grew older he realized his meager pension would never be able to cover his retirement expenses.

Initially he removed small amounts from travel funds. Before long, he started falsifying the payments to his network of spies. If he listed a payment of $1,000 dollars, it was actually only $500. It was so simple, why didn't anyone else think of it? *Then again, who's to say they didn't?*

Using this simple technique over a six-year period, Boris funneled $520,000 into a Swiss bank account. He then invested his money into the German and American stock markets. Netting a profit of $10.5 million by the time he withdrew his money in 2008.

Boris managed to walk only 75 to 100 feet from Peter before he paused in front of a large plate glass window that read "Styers Fudge" in gold and acrylic lettering. The window allowed Boris to view Peter in its reflection. He wanted to stick around to see what transpired with his young contact and maybe shadow him for an hour or two *just to see if he still had some of his old KGB skills.*

Boris watched Peter as he walked to a business no more than 50 feet from where he stood. *He must be replacing the pizza that he dropped when I scared the crap out of him,* thought Boris.

Boris scoured the crowd around him before noticing a man in a white dress shirt, minus the tie, put his hand to his ear, say something into his sleeve and walk to Mack & Manco's Pizza Shop.

Boris did not need to think twice, with FBI being his first thought. There were probably two or more agents spread out on the boardwalk with two or more in the rear of the shops and one on the beach. That would be typical for an FBI espionage operation.

That damn rookie slipped up somewhere thought Boris as he tried to blend in with the casually dressed crowd, assuming a position beside a young family of five. He walked in line with the young family as if he were part of their tight little group hoping to be assumed as the family's grandfather.

Boris strolled beside the family for a block or so before peeling off into one of the numerous Tee-shirt shops that plied their cheap wares along the boardwalk. Walking into one such shop, he quickly grabbed a hat boldly proclaiming, *"Ocean City is for lovers,"* a pair of aviator sunglasses, along with a black shirt that stated, *"Motorcycles rule the Beach."*

After paying the woman for his new attire, Boris promptly removed his old shirt, tossing it into a trash bin beside the cash register, and slipping on his new black one.

The older woman at the cash register blushed and turned away.

All for the better as she missed seeing the 9mm tucked into his waistband.

Boris adjusted his new hat, shirt and glasses in front of a small mirror at the shops exit. Satisfied with his new disguise he once again joined the masses on the boardwalk.

Boris walked for several blocks along the boardwalk before he spotted two men pushing their way through the crowds no more than 30 meters from his position.

Definitely FBI, thought Boris, *they were still wearing the suit coat in this oppressive heat. Did they all go to the same tailor?*

Boris turned away from his pursuers, searching for any possible avenue of escape. He spied a narrow alley only several meters away, ducking into the narrow walkway, breaking into a trot to try and put some distance between himself and his FBI pursers.

After 50 meters, he reached the end of the walkway dumping him into an even larger alley evidently used for trash pick-up.

Boris paused at the end of the alley before looking back to see his FBI pursuers now entering the same walkway, scrambling down towards his position in hot pursuit.

So much for his disguise.

Boris knew he could not compete with FBI agents 20 or 30 years younger than himself. He gathered what strength he could muster and jumped the remaining four steps to the alley below, landing cat-like on all fours, spraining his ankle in the process. Brushing himself off, he limped across the alley to a 24-hour laundry mat. Once safely inside, he positioned himself in the doorframe knowing his pursuers would soon make their appearance.

He didn't have to wait long as the FBI agents suddenly appeared, jumping down into the same alley in pursuit of their suspect.

Boris steadied his Glock 9mm against the door's wooden post before squeezing off two quick shots at his pursuers. The shots were purposely intended to miss. Boris just meant to intimidate the agents for the moment.

It had the desired effect.

Looking up from their exposed positions, the agents looked nervously to Boris as he walked to their position pointing his 9mm at one then the other.

Both agents cursed aloud.

"Gentlemen, I have no desire to see harm come to either one of you," Boris said as he walked closer to the men. "Please place your hands behind your neck and don't make any false moves or I will be forced to shoot you."

He moved to where the nearest agent lay, waiting for a response. "Come now, enough with being pissed at me. You are the ones who need retraining. First rule of pursuit, never jump into an unknown area or situation without performing a recon first." Boris reached in to remove the weapons from each of the agent's holsters.

"Still using the plastic Beretta? I recommend the Glock for maximum firepower." He held up his own weapon as evidence—waving it in front of their face as he shook his head. "Okay boys, now over to the dumpster." Boris pointed to a large green metal bin only yards away overflowing with the days refuse from the restaurant it served.

"Don't worry. I am not going to hurt you. I just need you in the dumpster to provide me with a little time to escape."

The smell of rotting food initially caused the Agents to hesitate.

Boris pointed his gun at the lead Agent.

Both quickly jumped in; settling in amongst the tomatoes, cardboard boxes and potatoes peels.

Boris held out his left hand. "Hand cuffs if you don't mind."

Boris used the first set of cuffs to snap each agent's hands together before taking the second set and connecting them to a metal rod on the outside of the trash bin.

"Ya'll have a nice day," Boris said in the best Texas accent he could muster.

As he was turning to leave, he thought better and walked back to where the agents stood chest high in the garbage. "Gentlemen, your keys for the hand cuff please."

Boris picked up his pace as he walked along Ocean Boulevard. He had to reach his car before the FBI back up team arrived on the scene.

With the drive to New York's Kennedy Airport taking almost 1-½ hours, he could still make his Swiss Air flight with hours to spare if he could evade the FBI.

Boris looked over his shoulder one last time, pressing on with the final hundred yards or so to the parking lot.

He could clearly see his rental car, right where he left it. The car was partially illuminated by the parking lots towering lights.

Boris eyed the area around his car. No FBI. No police. His curiously now piqued. He could slip into the parking lot virtually unnoticed and be on his way in a matter of minutes.

Boris removed his hat, shirt and 9mm and tossed them under a parked car as he continued walking. He decided to keep the glasses for another day. *No use wasting another $15.*

To the casual observer he was someone returning from a fun-filled day at the beach; shirtless, clad in shorts and sandals, only missing the dark socks older tourists seemed to prefer. He easily navigated the parked cars until he reached his own. He fumbled for a few seconds in locating his keys.

"Mister Boris Stevensky?" said an all too familiar voice from behind him.

His hands started trembling. Boris tried to ignore the voice.

"Mr. Boris Stevensky, could you please turn around with your hands in the air," the voice now commanded. "You are surrounded Boris, and I would hate to shoot you. Now, please do as I say."

Boris realized the predicament he was in, dropping his keys, slowly raising his hands as instructed. Three additional FBI agents surfaced from their hidden positions, guns trained on him.

"You!" Boris exclaimed as he turned to face an old nemesis from his Washington days, the voice now having a face. "I can't believe it. Is it really Mr. Michael Forsythe standing in front of me? I thought we killed you in Germany 15 years ago during a FSB shootout?"

Boris paused for a moment reflecting on what he had just said. *"Well, not me, but my old unit."*

Forsythe slowly shook his head. "No sir, as you can see I am still alive, Boris." Forsythe pulled up his shirt to reveal the scars where Russian bullets had once pierced his chest. Having operated as the FBI's Agent in Charge of Counter Intelligence for almost 30 years, his unit had personally thwarted over 23 terrorist actions. Each of the operations were coded "Top Secret" and not for public disclosure.

Unfortunately for Forsythe, he had reached mandatory retirement age and was only a few months away from the big day. The final few months on the job also meant desk duty.

Training his replacement and finishing loads of old case work. When word surfaced of an operation involving Boris Stevensky, he could not sit behind a desk and allow his field agents to nab this one. He personally commandeered the FBI jet that was always on 24/7 stand-by alert at Andrews Air Force Base, dragging along five of his best Counter-Intel agents in tow.

He was not about to miss one last duel with the Russians, *especially one involving his old KGB nemesis.*

"I'm impressed that you still remember me. I'm a little grayer in the hair and a few pounds heavier, but still the same Michael Forsythe as you can see." He walked over to Boris before frisking him. "From the embarrassment you caused our friends down the road here, I should put a bullet in your head right here and save our government the money of incarcerating you." Once finished, he leaned over to whisper in Boris's ear. "You're lucky we require you alive. Our superiors want you on TV, squealing like a pig, telling us all you know about your new acquaintances."

Boris smiled. "I don't know what you are talking about Michael. This has to be a misunderstanding on somebody's part. I was down here enjoying your nice American beach and its boardwalk. I have no reason to cause any trouble in your friendly country. I am a peaceful Russian citizen."

"You're slipping, Boris. Who said anything about you causing trouble?" Forsythe said, shaking his head in disappointment. "With you being a former instructor, you should have known better. Your own students would mock you if they could see you now. I am truly disappointed, Boris."

Forsythe motioned for his fellow agents to place him in a waiting car. "Get him out of my sight." He watched as his agents roughly heaved Boris into a blue sedan.

Forsythe retrieved his cell phone from his pocket, dialing a number from memory. As he waited for his contact to pick up, he looked around at the final stages of yet another magnificent sunset. He smiled at the similarities between his career and the sun, both basically in their final stages, but at least the sun would once again rise the next day.

When his contact picked up, Forsythe said. "Tracker, this is Jupiter. The planets are aligned."

CHAPTER SIX

Cape May, New Jersey

Peter had little trouble locating the bustling supermarket, *open 24 hours a day,* its banner proudly proclaimed—precisely where his Syrian handler said it would be.

He picked a spot on the right-hand side of the well-lit lot to park.

Retrieving his Koran from his overnight bag, he turned to the east and said his nightly prayers, thanking Allah for his good fortune. When he finished, he placed the Koran on his lap and reclined his seat, drifting off to sleep.

A car door closing roused him. He quickly checked his watch then re-checked the ferries schedule to confirm the departure times. Peter realized he had an hour to kill before boarding. He decided to drive to a local McDonalds for some breakfast. He had picked up a taste for Egg Mc Muffins during his short stay in the United States. He wondered how he would satisfy his craving when he returned home. His country had nothing similar to this decadence in America.

Driving to the parking lot's exit, he spied a local police car approaching from the opposite direction. Peter panicked for a split second until he saw the police officer turn his cruiser into the same McDonalds. Peter instinctively turned his car in the opposite direction. With his own breakfast plans on hold, he decided it would be prudent to head straight for the ferry. The presence of the police car suppressed any desire for food. His mission took precedence over his own needs; the needs of his people.

How selfish, he thought. *I have become contaminated by this American style of living after only three weeks.*

Spying the massive ferry from the road, Peter drove onto the gravel lot before noticing a cardboard sign haphazardly nailed to a wooden post proclaiming "ticket sales this way." Steering his vehicle in the direction of the crudely drawn arrow, Peter was able to spot a teenager who sported a roll of paper tickets almost the width of his skinny chest.

The line of cars in front of him was surprisingly short due to most of the vehicles having already pre-boarded. This being the busy summer season people wanted to be assured a space on the ferry. Some people even arrived two hours early to await boarding. Peter did not take this into account with his back-up plan. Luckily for him tickets were still on sale.

"One-way or roundtrip, sir," the lanky teenager said, leaning in on Peters rolled down car window for support. "$43 roundtrip or $25 one way," anticipating the question from Peter. He stood there looking back at the remaining cars in line, than to Peter.

"One way," Peter said, handing over the exact change, in return receiving a white paper ticket. *That was easy,* he thought as he drove forward, easing his car into the line as it snaked its way aboard the massive ferry. *Any other country would have police checking identification before boarding such a large ship. The lazy infidel Americans will soon learn the error of their ways. Everything would change after today.*

Peter maneuvered his car up the ten-meter wide steel ramp that announced the entrance to the ferry. At 25,000 Tons, the "Lady of the Delaware" was one of the largest car ferries operating in the lower 48 states. Peter carefully followed the uniformed workers hand signals that aligned his vehicle towards her center. After safely parking his car, Peter tuned his wheels inward as instructed by one of the ship's crew. He waited until they moved on to the next vehicle in line before silently praying to Allah for his good fortune. After several minutes, he finished his prayer, turning to see a woman of probably 70 or 80 years of age who just smiled at him as she proceeded to make the sign of the cross, obviously ending a short prayer herself. Peter waved to her.

After being cooped up all night in his car, Peter decided to walk topside. He also needed a suitable spot where the ships electronics would not interfere with a satellite phone call.

The top deck of the ferry lay crowded with passengers heading to the on-board coffee shop to feed their morning caffeine addiction. Peter decided to forgo the long line and walked to the stern of the ferry. He waited until the steel grated ramp was raised and locked in place.

Satisfied, Peter pulled out his satellite phone. He had to inform his superiors of their new status, *that of a nuclear power.*

CHAPTER SEVEN

Moscow, Russia - KARKOV Headquarters

Captain Isinov stood hovering over his prisoner, impatiently waiting for Sirna Miliriud to awaken from his drug-induced sleep. The Corpsman had provided him with just enough of the drug to sedate him for the 5-hour flight on a military aircraft from Grozny to Moscow. A dead captive would show poorly for his team's efforts. He looked to the clock once more before consulting his watch.

Captain Isinov motioned for the medical orderly to check Sirna's vital signs, this being the third time since he arrived only 30 minutes ago.

"Vital signs are normal, Captain," replied the elderly medical attendant. "His state of physical exhaustion could be causing the extended reaction.

Captain Isinov looked down on the rebel as he lay sleeping. *This man's days of wreaking havoc upon my fellow compatriots were over. This bastard was responsible for killing hundreds if not thousands of my countrymen. Soon he will betray his own troops and reveal to us the grand prize, their headquarters location.*

After several seconds of observing Sirna sleep, he turned curtly on his heels and paced from the room, realizing victory was finally appearing on the horizon.

CHAPTER EIGHT

Ocean City, New Jersey

Michael Forsythe nodded to his fellow Agents. "I want him taken to the local police station," he ordered the car's driver.

Forsythe then walked over to the second FBI car, leaning down to speak to his lead deputy, Alice Weatherspoon.

Alice was his "techie" of the group, able to accomplish things with a computer that others only dreamed of. If something were computer related, she could not only trace it, but also manipulate the information for their own use.

"Alice, we need to get this piece of shit talking or there might be trouble on our side of the pond. I want you to pull up the agency profile on our Russian friend and see what information we can use on this guy. You probably won't find anything nasty on him but check anyway. He might have slipped up somewhere in his travels. We need bank numbers, girlfriend's name, phone numbers; anything of value. Then, we need an isolated spot in the local police station, possibly a basement, so can put this gentleman through the ringer. Are you clear on where I'm going with this?"

"You got it boss," Alice replied, adjusting her black nylon vest that proclaimed FBI in big, bold, yellow letters on the front and back. "You want the man in the proverbial hot seat."

"You know the deal. And one more thing, I want you to have Rich and Jim contact their CIA counterparts over in Langley and see what they have on our boy. They must have a file as thick as a dictionary. Have them call in any overdue favors."

CHAPTER NINE

Aboard the "Lady Delaware"

Jim Cooper eased his seat back in his Ford F-150 pick-up truck listening to his scanner, hoping to pass the time by monitoring the local police radio frequency out of Cape May. It was known to be the busiest frequency along the coast due to the number of tourists who frequented Cape May for their summer holiday.

Jim hoped to do some surf fishing on the Delaware side of the bay for a change. A local had told him that perch were running into the lower bay. Lucky for him, his schedule with the Atlantic City police department afforded him with the luxury of two weeks of night work followed by two weeks of day work. This enabled him to indulge in his passion for surf fishing during the day, a time when most people were still chained to their desks. The night shift did possess one obvious downfall, a lack of quality sleep. Jim reclined his seat, hoping to catch some shut-eye before they reached the other side.

Jim was starting to doze off when two young kids ran by squirting water at each other with plastic water pistols, a squirt or two hitting Jim through his trucks open window. He laughed it off as he followed the children's progress as they ran to the bow of the ferry, using the cars for cover as they dueled.

Jim watched as the children run off.

Had it really been two years since the accident? Jim put his hands to his face, shaking his head. The police shrink had warned him certain events could be a trigger. His mind started to wander.

His wife Laura and his son Bobby were going to meet him for lunch. They tended to favor a local diner known for their meaty crab cakes, ones Laura loved to no end. Jim realized Laura's true motivation: to discuss their pending two-week vacation to England. She loved the picturesque English gardens and their stately museums and was determined to fit most of the majors into their itinerary. She said she only wanted to run a few things past him.

Changing something in her favor no doubt.

On the other hand, Jim and Bobby only wanted to catch some salmon in Northern England's Lake District. That was, if the *boss* approved and did not add yet another museum to their itinerary.

Deep down Jim realized she would eventually give her blessing after some minor give and take, mostly on his end.

Jim sat waiting patiently in a corner booth making small talk with the waitress, a friend from high school, when a call came in about an accident involving injuries only two blocks from the diner. Being the closest police officer to the scene, he had no choice but to respond. He knew Laura would chew his head off but deep down he also realized she would understand. *She always did.*

He was onsite within a minute. As Jim maneuvered his way through the crowd, he overheard a witness say that one of the cars involved in the accident had run a red light. Both vehicles involved in the accident were flipped over on their respective roofs with one lying sideways on top of the other, exposing their greasy underbodies. When he broke free of the crowd, Jim noticed the vehicle on the bottom was the same make and color as his wife's Ford Explorer. A sudden chill traveled down his spine upon realizing this was the same route she would drive.

Jim sprinted to the wreck, diving to the asphalt. He quickly crawled on his stomach in order to clear the vehicle on top. A strong odor of gasoline hung in the air. He knew he had to hurry before the whole area became an inferno. Using his nightstick as a hammer, he broke what remained of the back window, maneuvering his muscular frame into what normally would have been the back seat of their Ford Explorer, now crushed to half its size. He could hear a slight whimper from his wife faintly calling out his son's name. He could not see Laura with the truck's roof crushed down to front seat level, the seats joining together as one in the middle. Jim pushed his hand through a slight opening between the two front seats, reaching for where the voice was coming from. Once through, he could feel the silkiness of his wife's beautiful long brown hair, lightly stroking it. *I'm here baby,* he remembered saying, *everything is going to be okay. We are going to get you out real soon.*

Cramps forced him to pull his arm back; blood now covering his arm up to his elbow. *This can't be,* he cried aloud. *I'm going to get you out baby.* He used his nightstick to try and pry open the crumpled aluminum, struggling heroically in his fight to free them, all to no avail. *Finally, in desperation, he started clawing with his fingers.*

He remembered waking in an ambulance, a nurse carefully tending his hands where the sharp aluminum frame had sliced deep into his fingers.

The back doors of the ambulance lay propped open as if to provide a front row seat to view the carnage. Jim sat on the ambulance steps, slightly disoriented after being forcibly removed from the wreckage by his fellow officers who had appeared on the scene shortly after him. At first, he had struggled with his friends as they pulled him from the wreckage, finally collapsing in their arms.

Firefighters now worked the "Jaws of Life" to cut through the mangled mess, its hydraulic arms manipulating the steel and aluminum as if it were a child's toy. After several minutes, the front part of the Explorer lay open for all to see. The bodies of his wife and son positioned upside down, suspended only by their seat belts, life having drained from them long before.

Jim tried to rise but two of his fellow officers, friends from early childhood, restrained him.

He remembered crying out their names.

The drunk driver responsible for the accident stood beside the second ambulance, unscathed except for a cut he nursed on his head. Jim's fellow police officers forced the driver to watch the grisly scene as the firefighters cut the straps of the seat belts allowing the bodies to be lovingly caught as they dropped from their seats before being positioned side-by-side on the street. The driver tried to turn away from the carnage, but one of the police officers brutally twisted his head back to view the accident scene he alone had created.

And for Jim, what he had taken away.

Hit once again by an errant trail of water from the children's water guns, Jim's head snapped back in response, waking him from his dream like state as he watched the children run by once again through the ferries car deck. Jim didn't mind, the kids were only having fun. He wiped the small droplets from his check with his shirts sleeve. Was it water or tears? He was glad for the interruption, if only temporary.

Jim tried to find the Cape May Police department's frequency on his scanner. After some minor tuning, he heard Sergeant Allen's booming voice talking about the all you can eat rib dinner he had experienced the night before.

Allen is going to be the size of a car pretty soon, remembering the last time he saw Allen, he was pushing 250 pounds. Not too bad if you were 6 feet 5, but Allen was only 5 feet 10. *Leave it to him to find a good buffet.*

The Cape May dispatcher suddenly interrupted Sergeant Allen's conversation with another officer. "Attention all units in the vicinity of Route 9 south, between Ocean City and Cape May, we are on the lookout for a black, 2005 Impala. It's a rental car driven by a dark, Middle Eastern male, approximately 6 foot 1, average weight. He's wanted as an accessory for an assault on an FBI agent in Ocean City. He should be considered armed and dangerous. Call for back-up if sighted."

Caught off-guard by one of his law enforcement brothers being assaulted right in his backyard, Jim decided to check the ferry for the car. Hell, he still had almost an hour to kill before they arrived in Lewes, Delaware. If anything, it would allow the time to pass by earlier.

Reaching under his seat, Jim retrieved his 38 caliber snub nose, Smith and Wesson. Satisfied, he opened the glove box searching for his ammunition, something he always kept separate from his weapon. Once loaded, he stuck it in his pants waistline, pulling his denim shirt over his belt line to conceal the weapon. *It's probably a wild goose chase but what the hell; I need to take my mind off certain things anyway.*

Peter moved to the bow of the ferry two floors above the main car deck and thankfully away from the crowds. He had already informed his commander in Chechnya that mission success would be achieved within mere hours. His Commander then informed him that his close friend, Sirna, had disappeared several days before and was presumed to be dead or captured. If captured and in the hands of the Russian Security Service, it was only a matter of time before he would break and reveal the intimate details of Peter's plan.

Every minute now counted towards success.

Only a few more hours, and then all of America would feel his rage.

CHAPTER TEN

Ocean City, New Jersey

The single-story police building contained a narrow bank teller type cage that allowed the resident police sergeant to preside over all incoming traffic, buzzing them in when he so chose. A gray metal table and four accompanying chairs marked the extent of the spartan first floor. Used for the occasional suspect interrogation but mostly for the lucrative parking ticket franchise that most seasonal shore towns thrived on.

Forsythe nodded to the desk sergeant as he strolled with Boris in tow to the rear of the station, searching for the door to the basement.

The Sergeant looked up nonchalantly. "You can open the door; it leads down to the cell area. Same as I told the lady earlier."

"Thank you for your cooperation, Sergeant," Forsythe replied. "It should meet our immediate needs," grinning at Boris.

Forsythe decided it would be best if he questioned Boris in the basement area and away from the peering eyes of the local police establishment. Opening the door, he forcefully shoved Boris down the ten steps, watching as Boris hit every other step with either the back of his head or his face. Boris's battered body lay sprawled at the bottom in the fetal position, moaning.

Forsythe motioned for his fellow FBI agents to secure him to the single metal chair that occupied the first cell, using a combination of handcuffs and plastic wire-ties to accomplish the job.

"Sorry for the slippery steps, Boris," said Forsythe as he confidently strode around the chair where Boris sat.

"Michael, the cuffs are too tight," he protested. "They are breaking my wrists."

Forsythe merely laughed at him, waiting several minutes until his fellow FBI team members left the cell.

Forsythe now leaned down to eye level with his prisoner, tapping Boris on his head with his forefinger for emphasis. "Look at me Boris, focus on my face," he said.

Boris knew what was coming, mentally preparing himself.

Forsythe wasted no time, slapping him across the face, adding a bright red impression on his cheek to the diagonal gash over his left eyebrow from his fall down the steps. Boris protested once more: "I am still a Russian citizen, Michael. I would like to speak to someone at my embassy or consulate."

The blood now flowed freely from the cut above his eye, running down his cheek, dripping onto a white shirt the FBI had so kindly provided him. "I believe there is a consulate in Philadelphia that could provide answers concerning my diplomatic status."

Forsythe laughed aloud at his response, knowing full well that Boris was a wanted man on both sides of the ocean. The FBI wanted him almost as bad as his former employer, only the FSB put a $100,000 price on his head with the caveat being dead *or* alive. If he wanted to spar, Forsythe would go a single round. He needed the information Boris possessed. Lives were at stake; *American lives.*

Forsythe placed his cell phone in front of Boris. "You are right Boris, we should allow your country men to come pick you up and take you back to Mother Russia. I have the number if you would like to speak to your representative."

His bluff called, Boris slowly shook his head.

Forsythe took the phone back in response. "Honestly, do you think they would let a traitor like yourself live? I don't think so. They caught on to your little money scam several years back. Think about it you old spook, you're wanted *dead or alive. "*

Forsythe called his team back into the cell.

"I don't know what you are talking about Michael." Beads of perspiration blended with the blood trickling down from his forehead forming a crimson river that emptied onto his shirt. "You obviously have the wrong person."

Forsythe smiled at his captive before motioning for Alice to proceed with the information she was able to gather on Boris.

Alice hesitated due to the papers small print before she reached for her reading glasses. "Sorry boss, I'm getting up there in years like the rest of you old farts. Okay, this is what we have. Boris Stevensky; born in the Crimea, Soviet Union in

1945. Father was an Infantry Captain during WWII who was killed in 1945 during the battle for Berlin. In 1961, mother died of natural causes. In 1962, the KGB selected you from the Murmansk Sport Gymnasium for special training. You became a KGB operative starting in 1965. In 1970, you were sent to Paris for your first outside posting. In 1975, you arrived in Washington DC. While in Washington, you were a real bad boy, removing in excess of $500,000 dollars from an operations fund."

Forsythe cleared his throat.

Alice took the clue and stopped reading in deference to her boss.

"Boris, Boris, Boris," Forsythe laughed aloud. "What are we going to do with you? Let's regress a few years shall we? Remember that cute little blonde secretary you were very intimate with at your embassy in 1977? The one *your own people* brought over from Moscow due to the paranoid security concerns within your Embassy? Well, grab onto your boots for this one, Boris. She worked for us. We turned her many years before with the lure of American hard currency. So in a way, she was similar to you with her infatuation with the almighty dollar. One difference, she played you like a Steinway piano, my boy. She knew every move you made and relayed the information back to us."

They had him.

Forsythe turned his back on Boris, walking over to where Alice now sat. "Sorry for the interruption, Miss Weatherspoon, please do continue."

"Yes, where was I?" Searching for where she had left off, she removed her glasses then put them back on again. "Okay, here we go. Our little communist friend here has turned capitalist. He invested his new-found monies into a diversified stock portfolio split between both the US and German Stock Markets, creating a net profit of over $10 million by 2008."

Boris scoffed at them, laughing aloud, shaking his head, realizing he had the opportunity to get one jab in before they ruined him. "No, it was 2006 to be exact, Miss Weatherspoon. If you are going to get it right, please adjust your records to indicate 2006," he replied sarcastically. Boris looked around the room at each of the assembled agents, nodding politely. "All right, you have me. I cancel my request to speak to the Russian Consulate. Needless to say, I do not wish to see my Russian friends. No need to make them aware of my presence. They thought my disappearance several years back meant poor Boris was dead. No need for them to think any differently."

"You are right about that, Boris. I never dialed the number anyway, that would be too tacky on my part." He knew Boris was about to provide them something valuable, so he kept prodding. "Your government would confiscate your cash and kill you and every member of your family that still walks this earth. You know that, and I know that. Your people are a ruthless bunch of assholes." He walked back to where Boris sat allowing one of his fingers to interrupt the trickle of blood that flowed down his face, holding it in front of Boris before choosing to wipe it on his already bloodied, white shirt.

Agent Knox took the signal from his boss, lighting a cigarette, placing it in Boris's mouth, allowing him to take a drag.

Boris thanked him with a nod. "Nothing like a good cancer stick to calm the nerves." A smile revealed a solid silver front tooth. "To answer one of your questions, Michael, we have been invaded many times, so please do not cast judgment on something you have never experienced. Our country lay decimated the last time foreign troops invaded and tread upon our soil. The German Army destroyed everything for over a thousand miles in each direction. From this we became a, as you said so eloquently, '*a ruthless bunch of assholes.*' Throw in Attila and Stalin, and yes, we have the scent of blood on our hands. Only we seek revenge for unjust actions. What's your excuse?"

Forsythe had no desire to spar with the Russian; he was too cagey for that. He allowed Boris to become relaxed before striking out once more. Basic psychology; a trick his old instructors taught him well. Beat them down for a certain amount of time before allowing a small window of opportunity to open, hence the cigarette and the polite history lesson.

Casting off his friendly demeanor, Forsythe slapped him harshly across the face before delivering a blow to his stomach. Boris doubled over in agony as he struggled, gasping for air.

"Okay, Boris, we've had our fun now let's cut to the chase. What did you pass to your little friend? What was in the envelope? Speak up, Boris. I don't want to have to start on your ribs."

Forsythe realized he was getting too old for this sort of work as he rubbed his hand wondering if he had broken something of his own.

Boris straightened up in his chair, still gasping for air, but not wanting to provide his captors the satisfaction of knowing the extreme pain he was in. "If I were to speak," he said, pausing to catch his breath."I want a deal. Promise me that much. Will you allow me to keep what I have earned for any information you may receive?" He anticipated some type of bargain to be struck. But he also recognized the particularly dire situation he was in.

Forsythe smiled. "Are you kidding me? What the hell do you think this is? We could kill you, dump your body in the ocean and nobody would know or even give a damn."

Agent Knox walked up the steps to make sure the door was closed and locked, not wanting the Ocean City Police to have a sideshow.

Boris looked straight ahead, mentally reviewing his options, finding none to his liking. His only chance would be to feed the FBI small bits of information and feign the rest. Maybe, just maybe, they would let him go with some type of deal.

Boris wanted to be out of the country before Peter made it to Washington.

If not, he was a dead man.

CHAPTER ELEVEN

Aboard the Lady Delaware

Jim walked about the ferry's main car deck, looking for any signs of the suspect's car. A Police Officer for 11 years, he knew people panicked in the heat of the moment, so he made a concentrated effort to check all black vehicles. In Jim's line of business, he had to be aware of all makes and models. There was no room for mistakes on a vehicle description in his book.

While strolling the main deck, Jim came up with what he thought would be an excellent idea for law enforcement. Run a check of all license plates on the cars as they boarded the ferry. By the time the ferry docked almost two hours later, they could have identified any potential scofflaws or criminals. *The ACLU would have a field day on that one*, Jim thought.

Carefully navigating down the narrow lanes between the vehicles, he noticed cell phones, suitcases, even wallets lying out on the front seats. It constantly amazed Jim how many people left their vehicles unlocked with valuables in clear sight for all to see. *What do they think? Because they were on a ferry, all crime takes a holiday? People will never learn.*

Passing the midway point of the car deck, a hint of marijuana hung in the air as he passed a rusting, lime green, 2003 Toyota. Its middle-aged occupants had the windows rolled up and were enjoying the partial ocean view the ferry provided as they happily puffed away, oblivious to anyone around them. Jim walked right past the couple. He didn't have the time to squash their fun, for two cars in front of the Toyota he noticed his prey.

His reflexes took over as he approached a black, 2005 Impala. Patting his waistband for his 38, he proceeded to the rear bumper of the vehicle. From where he stood, he could view the complete interior of the vehicle. Satisfied no one was still in the vehicle, he walked to the driver's side of the car. *Let me just see if the car door is open,* looking from side-to-side for any potential witnesses, only viewing the middle-aged couple smoking pot two cars away, still oblivious to the world around them. Jim cautiously tugged at the handle, preparing to walk away if an alarm sounded. Not completely surprised, he found the door unlocked.

He quickly slipped into the vehicle.

Jim sat in the driver's seat for a few moments wondering what in the hell he was doing? Breaking and entering would get him removed from the force if caught. *You only live once,* he said aloud, leaning over and opening the glove compartment. He removed its contents and spread them on the passenger seat in plain view. He picked through the assorted fast food wrappers, candies, maps and finally, a rental car agreement. Jim chose to start with the rental agreement. He found it registered to a Peter Zarinsko, writing down the name on a piece of paper. The maps were for the Washington DC and Philadelphia areas. He didn't find anything else that might provide any clues before placing everything back in its place in the glove compartment and exiting the car.

Peter fed the seagulls some of his left over French fries. The seagulls were fighting an aerial duel above him, each jostling for position before swooping in three at a time to feed upon the greasy food, oblivious to their cholesterol levels like their human counterparts. After emptying the remaining contents into the sea below him, Peter could see the outline of Lewes, Delaware before him.

Two loud blasts from the ferries horn informed everyone of the ferry's intention of docking.

Walking down the crowded metal stairway to the vehicle deck, he noticed a tall white male exiting his vehicle. "What the hell," Peter said aloud, startling the older couple walking in front of him.

The woman provided him with a nasty scowl.

Peter finally broke free of the main crowd as the stairway suddenly widened allowing him to run down the remaining steps with the speed of a gazelle. He effortlessly moved past the three rows of cars positioned along the base of the steps until stopping at his own car. Peter stood for a moment watching Jim jog back to his own vehicle. There was no time to chase after the man, for they were pulling into port.

Peter quickly entered and closed the door of his car. He had nothing of value in the car. Maybe some change from the tollbooths, looking to see that it was still in the ashtray. He then opened the glove compartment checking to see that his rental documents and maps were intact, satisfied they were, he slammed it shut.

It has to be the FBI, he said aloud.

Peter checked under the front seat of his car locating his weapon, removing it and laying the weapon within arm's reach. He recited a quick prayer, finishing in time to watch the ferry as it slowly inched its way into the Lewes city dock.

If it is a fight you desire, I am more than willing to oblige.

With the lowering of the ferries drawbridge, tens of cars all started their engines in unison. Adjusting his rear view mirror Peter suspected his adversary would call in the car's location and allow Peter to be "handed-off" to another FBI or unmarked police vehicle. He would have to deal with this possibility and quickly.

He was only hours away from accomplishing his mission and no one was going to interfere, not at this stage.

Jim started back to his own vehicle, leaving the suspect's car virtually untouched except for the glove compartment. Retracing his steps past the middle-aged pot smoking couple, now evidently feeling more relaxed by the combination of pot and the gentle rocking motion of the ferry. Jim noticed the man calmly point back to the car he had just broke into and silently mouth *shame, shame* to him, waging his finger at him in jest. This caused his wife to burst out in an uncontrollable fit of laughter.

Who else noticed? He looked over his shoulder at the car, seeing nothing out of the ordinary. He scanned the group of people now coming down the steps from the topside lounge area. The group contained mostly white, elderly tourists heading for a tour bus, included among this group was a well-tanned man with dark hair.

He was staring right at Jim.

Jim picked up his pace. *I have to get back to my truck and call this in.*

CHAPTER TWELVE

Nakyata Pass, Chechnya

The Chechnya Mujahedeen Headquarters lay situated deep within a pristine pine forest preserve along the valley floor of the Nakyata Pass. The area lay blessed with a virtual carpeting of pine trees that seemingly towered one over the other. Their sheer size provided a jungle like canopy, with the suns bright rays barely able to penetrate to the moss covered ground below.

The Headquarters location posed somewhat of a mystery to the Russian military, having never been betrayed nor observed by any Russian forces that eagerly sought its existence. Most of those same troops thought its existence to be mere fiction. Others knew better.

Naturally camouflaged from Russian surveillance aircraft, the headquarters for the Rebel Army was a highly sought after prize by the Russian government. If they could capture the facility or even destroy it, they might be able to end the rebellion in one swift maneuver. This was motivation enough for the Russian government, the war already costing them over 10,000 Russian soldiers killed or wounded in battle.

At present, the area contained a defending force of only 150 men and women whose job alternated between loading equipment and being ever vigilant for the marauding Russian forces.

One man ambled the gravel path between two of the wooden "residence huts," fingering his prayer beads as he received heartfelt greetings from all who passed by. As head of the rebel resistance movement, Omar Turhaniz was deeply saddened by the disappearance of his second in command, Sirna Miliruid. His sudden disappearance only increased the burdens and pressures placed upon him.

Omar knew the possibility existed that the Russians had captured Sirna. Not wanting to take any unnecessary chances, Omar authorized the evacuation of his headquarters complex. He ordered his small staff to retreat 10 kilometers west of their present location, to a cross roads near the old market town of Goltea. They would retreat to a network of limestone caves first excavated on orders by Stalin in 1942.

Omar took time away from the main hustle and bustle of the evacuation, rubbing his graying beard as he contemplated Sirna's situation. When first informed of his disappearance, Omar deployed as many men he could spare, virtually saturating the area with his freedom fighters, disbursing them in all directions searching for any possible clues. For over 12 hours, his troops combed the area surrounding the ambush site, finally reaching the conclusion he had indeed been captured. Omar ordered the troops to not speak of Sirna's capture, fearing the remainder of his forces knowing the truth. His troops held Sirna in high esteem, cherishing his leadership skills and lion-hearted bravery. Omar preferred to let his troops continue thinking that Sirna died fighting bravely in battle; only his body had yet to be located. No need to let them think otherwise.

Omar's primary concern for the moment lay with Peter's mission in the United States.

Once Peter fulfilled his mission, the Americans would have no choice but to enter our war, on our side.

Just as planned.

CHAPTER THIRTEEN

Moscow, Russia - KARKOV Headquarters

Speaking hurriedly into his cell phone, Captain Isinov informed his commanding general on the situation with Sirna.

"Yes sir, our prisoner is awake as we speak. May I be so bold to recommend we alert our bomber forces to proceed to a stand-by status with a three hour alert?"

The General obviously concurred as he allowed the captain to continue.

"Comrade General, the medical staff has informed me that it will take several minutes for the drugs to have the desired effect and work its way through his system. I will call you the moment he discloses the headquarters location."

Captain Isinov hung up the phone. He walked over to where Sirna lay restrained with metal hand and foot cuffs, awaiting the arrival of the staff doctor.

"How is our patient today?" Captain Isinov said, having changed into his full dress uniform, displaying four rows of service ribbons for combat military actions in Afghanistan, Angola and now Chechnya. He hoped to intimidate his prisoner in some perverse way.

Captain Isinov mocked Sirna's conditions, laughing as he grabbed the leg restraints, pulling on the metal chain that held his legs affixed to the standard Government Issue hospital bed.

"Are you enjoying our Russian hospitality?" Captain Isinov said.

The prisoner chose not to respond, staring overhead at the white tiled ceiling, redirecting and channeling his anger for the moment.

Captain Isinov moved around to the opposite side of his bed, taking time to smooth the white cotton sheet that Sirna lay upon. He sat down on the bed beside him.

Sirna closed his eyes for several seconds to garner some inner strength. *The infidels had no idea their world was about to come crashing down about them.* Opening his eyes, he stared at the captain as if he were the devil himself, focusing on the man's narrow eyes for the first time noticing one was brown and the other blue. *He knew it. A sign of the evil that lay within.* If captured by one of his freedom fighters, they would pluck his eyes out then burn him alive.

"In a raspy voice, speaking for the first time since captured, Sirna said: "What do you want from me?"

Captain Isinov rose from the bed. "Ah, the man has a voice after all. A bit dry from the drugs that we have provided to you, but clear still the same."

He walked over to where his medical assistant stood in the room's doorway with an older, gray haired man. "Please come in, Comrade Doctor. I would like to introduce you to our VIP," he said sarcastically. "Introductions are in order. Mr. Sirna Miliruid, please meet the esteemed, Doctor Razinski, of our humble Medical Institute. Our Doctor Razinski works for the Russian military establishment here at the Institute, specializing in the technique of extracting information from prisoners such as yourself. He was kind enough to come here today to assist in our conversation. From what I hear he can be quite persuasive."

The Captain eyed Sirna, waiting for his reaction. Sensing none, he continued. "Doctor if you would be so kind as to lay your tools of the trade on the table, we can proceed."

Sirna ignored the doctor as he dropped his black medical bag on the table. Wasting no time, Doctor Razinski started removing odd shaped metal tools from inside the bag laying them on a table beside Sirna in a neat row according to size. He smiled nervously down at Sirna. "Today is your lucky day, Sirna Miliruid. You are to be the first test case for a new version of a truth serum we have developed right here at our Institute."

The doctor turned to the captain with a questionable look upon his face. "That is if the captain allows me to proceed?" He pointed to a needle and syringe. "Then again, he may have some other interesting ideas?"

The captain had enough of the doctor's toying. He wanted the process to begin as soon as possible.

Captain Isinov brushed aside the petite doctor, approaching his display of tools, selecting a stainless steel surgical scalpel with a one-centimeter blade. He held the scalpel up to the ceiling light, waiting until the stainless steel blade reflected its rays into Sirna's eye, blinding him for a second or two.

"Thank-you doctor, that will all for the moment," the Captain said.

"Sirna, I would like to start by asking you a few questions. Now, you can choose to ignore them, or you can provide me with the answers I require. It's your decision."

With blade in hand, Captain Isinov slowly sliced the green hospital robe that Sirna wore, cutting its thin fabric from his knees up to his chin.

Sirna started his evening prayer not realizing what time of day it was, asking Allah to provide him with the strength to withstand the torture that would surely come.

Captain Isinov looked back to the doctor in disbelief.

When his prayers ended, Sirna screamed aloud, "Allah Akbar."

Captain Isinov jumped back in response, startled for the moment, quickly recovering as he moved the scalpel to within inches of Sirna's eyes, allowing him to see the sharpness of the stainless steel blade.

"Enough with the pleasantries. Let us start with an easy question shall we? Where is the location of the Rebel Headquarters, Sirna?" He pushed the sharp end of the blade into the soft tissue above Sirna's right eye, blood now flowing freely.

"I am not a monster, just a plain soldier like yourself. I only want to know certain pieces of information, and then I will leave you to your God."

He moved the blade to the left eye. "Shall we start again? Let us be reasonable men, Sirna. Where is the location of the Rebel Headquarters?"

He waited several seconds before plunging the blade into the skin above the left eye.

A shriek escaped from Sirna's lips, sounding as if he were a wounded animal. Crimson liquid covered both of his eyes now, his eyelids fluttering uncontrollably. He begged Allah to take him as he struggled against the chains that bound him to the metal-framed bed.

"Your God cannot help you here, Sirna, only I can stop the pain." He put his hand over Sirna's mouth to stop his prayer from being overheard. "Tell me what I want to know and I will see that you are taken to a proper medical facility for treatment."

He scouted for a new instrument of pain, settling on a claw hammer. "They will repair the nerve damage above your eye so you can still lead a normal life."

"I am not enjoying watching your life slowly drain away from you, Sirna."

He grabbed Sirna's right foot, pushing up his leg so the foot lay flat on the table. "Where is the location of the Rebel Headquarters? I will keep asking the same question over, and over again. I will have no choice but to break every bone in your body if you do not respond." He waited several seconds before sensing no response was forth coming. He raised the hammer before slamming it on his large toe, the force of the blow undoubtedly shattering the bone into tiny fragments.

Sirna passed out from the intense pain.

Captain Isinov slapped the man repeatedly, trying to revive him. Seeing no response, he used the hammer to smash the remainder of his toes on the right foot.

"If he lives, he will never walk again," said Captain Isinov with a grin upon his face.

Captain Isinov placed the hammer gently back on the table where the doctor's assorted tools lay, trying to control his anger, remembering how many of his countrymen had died due to rebels like Sirna.

"I don't want to continue like this. It's not right. I'm sinking to the level of this bastard. I am a professional soldier, not a murderer. It is time for the new truth serum, comrade doctor. This man is as tough as a Siberian plow horse."

With that, he relinquished the reins of the interrogation to the doctor.

Doctor Razinski walked over to where his assortment of tools that lay spread on the table, selecting the plastic syringe and needle as his weapon of chose. He then searched his medical bag for the glass vial of serum, absentmindedly locating it in his lab coat pocket.

"Elusive little thing," holding the vial up for the Captain to see. "This will relax our friend to the point of him experiencing no pain whatsoever. He will feel as though he were drifting on a cloudbank. We will be able to start the interrogation within seconds of the cool liquid flowing into his veins."

The captain smirked at the prospect of an interrogation without some type of pain levied on a prisoner. "You have to make them feel something, comrade doctor, so they will remember and tremble from your mere footsteps walking down the hall."

The doctor nodded. "I would have agreed with you until this miracle drug came along and replaced our old sodium pentothal. With sodium pentothal, a prisoner could resist to a point where some type of torture might be necessary. Times change."

Captain Isinov slapped Sirna across his blood-smeared face. Damn it, wake up you little shit!" He then proceeded to slap him only harder.

Sirna still lay unconscious upon the bed.

"Raising his hand for the fifth time, caught in mid-air by a thick-armed barrel of a man from behind, Captain Isinov reacted by swinging his left hand in the direction of the man. Again, the fist caught in mid-flight by the same powerful man.

Captain Isinov quickly realized his mistake. "Sir, my apologies," he said, snapping to attention. "I was not aware it was you, General Poszk; please forgive me."

As Commander in Chief of all Russian Special Forces, including the KARPOV Group, General Poszk was Captain Isinov's boss. The General maintained the utmost respect for Captain Isinov even though he personally reduced him in rank three times over the past 14 years for conduct unbecoming an officer. Captain Isinov would have been Colonel Isinov with a good chance to receive his Generals strip if he had kept his nose clean.

He placed his hand around Captain Isinov's shoulders, leading him out of earshot from the doctor and his medical assistant. "Captain Yuri Isinov, why don't we allow the good doctor to apply his medical treatment to the prisoner and see if he will be more cooperative? I might need someone of your expertise to lead the attack on the Rebel Headquarters when this is finished. We need this prisoner alive and well. No more slicing and dicing, okay? We might be able to use him in a prisoner exchange for some of our boys.

Captain Isinov knew he reacted partly out of frustration. He wanted to end the war himself and saw this prisoner as an excellent opportunity to do so. "Comrade General, I must apologize for my behavior. I know how much you have protected my career. You could have chosen to dismiss someone like myself many years back, and I thank you for not doing so." He looked the General straight in the eye, and then took his hand in friendship.

"All right then, let's get back to work," the General said, slapping him on the back, both walking back to where the prisoner lay motionless.

"Comrade Doctor, is our prisoner ready to unburden himself with the details of the remaining rebel secrets?"

Doctor Razinski stood beside the general, monitoring the pulse of his weary patient. He had provided the truth serum to Sirna only two minutes ago watching as it quickly took its desired effect.

"General, the time has come. He should be under the drugs influence. You may proceed with your questioning at any time."

The General dismissed the doctor and his medical assistant from the room before motioning Captain Isinov to take up a position on the opposite side of the hospital bed. They both stood solemnly at Sirna's bedside, waiting to hear the metallic click of the door closing.

"Do you know anything about the man we have here, Yuri? Any details on his life? Anything private?"

"Yes, sir," he said, reaching into his dress shirt, extracting a yellow piece of paper. "We have a one page dossier on our man, all of it documented and verified by our FSB."

The general quickly scanned the sheet before handing it back to the captain. "Very good. Ask him a few personal questions to see if we are on the right track. This will be our test case to see if he is telling us the truth."

Captain Isinov briefly consulted the sheet of paper looking for some easy questions. "Sirna, can you hear me?"

A soft "Yes," was his response.

"Where were you born, Sirna?" said Captain Isinov as he leaned over him, carefully wiping the blood from around his eyes, allowing him to briefly view his captors.

Sirna lay motionless on the bed. A feeling that he was completely at rest suddenly overwhelmed him. He had never experienced such a feeling. It felt as though his body were floating on a cloud. The only thing that troubled him was the fact that he was not in control of his body; it was choosing its own path. *Is this paradise? Was he already dead and preparing to meet, Allah? Yes, it had to be. Only Allah could make such words want to flow so freely from his mouth.*

"I was born in the village of Kirnez, oh great one," Sirna said, a smile appearing on his face thinking Allah was standing over him.

Captain Isinov nodded to the general. He continued. "Sirna, what position do you presently occupy in the Rebel Army?"

"I am presently the Eastern District Commander in Chechnya."

The general signaled for the captain to proceed with the tougher questions, wanting answers before anything happened to Sirna in his weakened state. The serum was known to cause heart attacks in some patients.

"Sirna, when captured by the Russian soldiers you were coming from your headquarters. Can you tell us the location of your headquarters?"

Sirna wavered as he resisted with the answer, grunting and straining against the chains on his hands and legs, sweating profusely, finally relenting when his head eased back unto the pillow. The floating effect had stopped. "From the spot of capture, it was close to four and ½ kilometers south by south east," he spat out in disgust.

General Poszk removed a detailed ordinance map from his briefcase, spreading it out on the same table occupied by the doctor's instruments. "The red x marks where we captured him, so that would place the headquarters right about here," pointing to the Nakyata Pass. "Show this map to him; get him to pinpoint the location of the Headquarters."

The captain wiped the blood from Sirns's eyes then held the detailed map up for Sirna to see. "Sirna, can you show us the location on this map? We need to know the Headquarters position."

Sirna felt groggy from the drug's effects, trying to focus on the map as the captain eagerly held it for him. He tried to fight the impulse to speak aloud but his tongue and brain were working in defiance. "In the valley of Nakyata, partially buried in a cliff. It has a rock outcropping that resembles a rams ear."

"The rams ear?" repeated Captain Isinov, looking at the map himself, walking around the bed with the map and over to the general. "If we go south 4½ kilometers it would bring us to this location." His finger traced along the route. "It would obviously be somewhere off the trail over here in the mountainous area bordered by the tree line. The valley of Nakyata, that is right here, one kilometer from the trail."

"Here, right here," the General said excitedly. "It resembles an ear of a sheep or ram, right here." He pointed to the spot on the map for the captain to observe before thrusting the map in front of Sirna for concurrence.

The captain wiped the blood from above Sirna's eyes allowing him to view the map. "Yes, that is the position." *He could not distinguish if it were Allah or the devil who now controlled his tongue.*

Still not satisfied, the general continued. "We are not complete here, Yuri. This man still has more information to provide us." He picked up the yellow piece of paper in his search for additional questions.

"May I proceed with some questions of my own, sir?" Captain Isinov said.

"By all means Yuri, please."

"Thank-you, sir," said Captain Isinov before turning his attention to the captive. "Sirna, when the Russian officer captured you, where were you heading? What was your mission?"

"That man was evil," Sirna spit out, again straining against the chains that bound him to the bed. "He killed my brother in front of my own eyes. The heavens cannot hold me. I will seek revenge upon that man!"

"It is okay my friend," he replied. "He will soon have to pay his own price. Please answer the question I posed to you."

Sirna smiled. "I was leading a patrol to the front lines of our glorious troops to inform them of our impending victory." He relaxed as he thought he was still walking amongst his troops. "We have procured two weapons of mass destruction and are in the process of using them against our enemies. Victory will soon be ours."

The general dropped the cigarette he was lighting along with its accompanying lighter onto the floor, allowing the hollow metallic click of the lighter to resonate throughout the room. A look of shock spread across his face. "Did I hear him correctly? Did he just say a weapon of mass destruction?"

"No, sir, he said *weapons*. Plural."

"Ask him for more details before he comes around and the drug's effect wears off."

Captain Isinov once again wiped the blood from around Sirna's eyes, causing him to stammer a slight "thank-you" in response.

"Sirna, what are you referring to when you say weapons of mass destruction?"

Sirna laughed aloud as if a spirit had taken hold of his badly bruised body. Looking first to Captain Isinov, then to the general, eying both as if they were the last to know about the secret mission.

"I speak of the two nuclear weapons our comrades have secured in the United States."

The general's eyes went wide. "Where are the exact locations of the weapons and who has them Sirna?"

"One of our brave freedom fighters has found two nuclear weapons. He will use them to destroy Washington DC and Philadelphia."

Sirna started foaming about the mouth, convulsions setting in.

The general tried to hold Sirna down on the bed, Sirna strained against the chains. "Get the doctor in here!" he shouted.

The doctor ran over to where the general held Sirna down. "This man is experiencing a massive coronary," he glanced at his medical assistant, knowing the drug was to blame.

"Katherine, get the electric paddles from room two! Hurry!"

"A potent but evil side effect," the doctor said in-between counting and pressing down heavily on Sirna's now silent chest. He stopped after several minutes to seek a pulse, pressing two fingers against Sirna's neck searching for the main artery. He shook his head as he looked at the general.

"You tried your best, comrade doctor," the General said in response. "We have all the information we require."

The General and Captain Isinov bid a hastily retreat from the room. Once they were clear, the general looked up and down the hallway before speaking. "The bombing will begin in several hours, followed up by a surgical insertion of KARPOV with assistance from regular army soldiers."

Captain Isinov suddenly realized he would be missing one of the last, important battles of the war.

The General nodded to him. "For you, I have another mission, which if successful, could save a potential conflict between Russia and our old adversary."

Ever the obedient soldier, Captain Isinov stared straight ahead, ready for his new orders.

"You are going to the United States."

CHAPTER FOURTEEN

Aboard the Lady Delaware

Jim Cooper started his car and immediately reached for his Motorola scanner hoping to get in touch with the FBI. He repeatedly pressed the scanner's transmit button but the light would not change from red to green. *I don't believe this*, banging the unit with his fist to see if he could persuade the unit to transmit.

He noticed the cars around him were beginning to slowly inch forward. Jim eyed the suspects Ford Impala as it inched its way towards the ramp no more than 200 feet in front of his vehicle. *I guess it's up to me to follow this guy before he gets away.* He cursed silently for not bringing along his cell phone.

Exiting the ferry, Jim made a right hand turn, driving 200 yards to the first intersection. He searched the area looking for the suspect's car. While waiting for the light to change, he noticed the suspect's car stuck at a traffic intersection only two blocks ahead.

Little did Jim realize but Peter was already moving towards his first destination, *Washington DC*.

CHAPTER FIFTEEN

Lewes, Delaware

Peter decided it would be best to keep away from the main section of town, approaching the more rural part of Lewes. *That is where I shall meet the man trailing behind me.* He drove confidently down the nearly deserted highway, wondering if he would have to use his weapon that now lay beside him. Looking in his rear view mirror, he could see the black pick-up truck no more than 100 meters back with only two cars physically separating them. The officer tried his best to stay out of sight, angling his vehicle so it would be positioned directly behind the one in front. *This man certainly knew his business.*

Peter picked up the Road Atlas he purchased in Philadelphia, opening the book to find a map of Delaware. Placing it on the steering wheel as he drove, alternating between searching the road for traffic and then the map for his location. He tried to find a possible ambush site ahead of him, locating a State Park Game Land only two miles away. Looking in his rearview mirror, he noticed that the black pick-up was now the single vehicle trailing behind him, the others having already turned off the road.

Excellent. I can move this game into the forests where I will be the hunter.

A roadway sign to his right announced that for the next three miles the road would consist of a series of hairpin turns. A smile creased Peter's face, knowing that only Allah could have provided such divine assistance.

Peter safely negotiated the first turn a good 20 miles an hour over the posted speed limit. Once out of the turn he sped up, allowing all 6-cylinders to kick in. He hoped to put some distance between the trailing officer and himself, seeing his opportunity approach via a 150-meter straightaway before the next set of turns.

A large green and brown sign on the side of the road proudly proclaimed that he had entered the Arnold J. Black State Game Lands.

Peter peered in his rear view mirror only to notice that the truck had yet to come out of the first turn. *He should have been there by now with the rate of speed he was driving. Something's wrong. Is he holding back? Were his fellow officers lying in wait just ahead? Is he "pushing" me into a trap?*

The distance between them steadily increased to over 300 meters.

This was the break Peter was waiting for as he steered confidently into the second turn, and once again allowing the speedometer to reach 20 miles over the posted limit. He had the distance and surprise. Eyeing the road ahead, Peter spotted what appeared to be a dirt road on his right. He tapped his brakes several times before pulling up on the emergency brake, his car swerving in reaction; this allowed Peter to maneuver his car into the turn and onto the dirt road sending a cloud of dust and rock into the air.

Potholes swiftly introduced themselves. They were small at first, only to be greeted further down the road by larger ones. After several near misses, his car bottomed out on a hole whose impact caused two of the car's tires to burst with a loud pop.

Peter had no choice but to continue driving, for he had to pick the spot of his ambush, not his pursuer.

Jim maintained a respectable distance behind the suspect's car on the nearly empty road, with most of the ferry traffic heading north to the outlet malls that lined the shoreline. But not his prey, he headed west away from the hustle and bustle of the area. Jim followed suit, trailing his suspect as he drove off the main drag and out of town.

Peter allowed one car to separate them. Using a car as a buffer made it was easier to tail a suspect as long as they maintained the same speed as the suspect's car. If the buffer car moved at a slower speed then the suspect's car, he risked the possibility of losing the suspect's vehicle in the process. This would force him to pass the slower vehicle and chance exposing himself.

The gray hair and small profile of the woman driving ahead of him provided Jim with no sense of assurance.

He had already passed several payphone's but wisely decided to remain behind his suspect. He banged his scanner with his fist for the third time since departing the ferry. "Piece of junk," he said aloud.

Looking down at his trucks odometer, he noticed they had driven almost seven miles outside of Lewes. It would be easier for someone of his ethnic background to blend into a city environment instead of the relatively flat country of southern Delaware. *It was all farmland out here. Was he possibly meeting someone?*

The older woman in front of Jim surprised him by keeping pace with the suspect's car just in front of her, feeling guilty about profiling her.

Her right turn signal now blinking, she turned into the entrance to a farm that sat off the main road.

Jim now lay exposed. *It won't take long before he becomes aware I'm here.* He decided to ease his truck back another couple hundred feet hoping not to spook the suspect.

Jim estimated 400 feet separated him from the suspect's car as he turned into a bend in the road. He slowed his truck to the recommended speed for the turn, completing the turn in time to see the suspect's car already entering the next set of curves. Jim sped up to close the distance in the straightaway. Approaching the next bend, he down clutched to ease his truck into the turn before coming out to yet another straightaway. His view was unobstructed for a mile or so, but the suspect's car had suddenly vanished. Jim noticed a dirt road to his right. That would be his only choice besides the highway. Jim ignored the dirt road, choosing to stay on the highway. He could always return if he didn't locate the suspect up ahead.

After two miles of high-speed driving, Jim's truck exited the state game lands and came upon another yet another straightaway, this one providing an unobstructed view for several miles. The suspect's was car nowhere to be seen.

Jim realized the terrible mistake he had made, performing a quick 360-degree turn. He put his foot to the floor, attaining 65 in the turns, 95 on the straightaway, reaching the dirt road in a matter of minutes. Jim drove down the dirt road with reckless abandon; his truck easily absorbing the potholes that had flattened Peters tires. Jim looked for any signs of a dust cloud that would announce his suspect's presence, the heavy canopy of pine trees providing him no help. After several miles he slowed his truck down to a more manageable speed, not wanting to wrap his truck around a tree. He also didn't want to drive into an ambush that may lie around any of the roads numerous turns.

The thrill of the chase made think back to a refresher course he had taken at the Police Academy several weeks before. His instructor taught him a new technique for chasing criminals in the forested areas; at least it was new to the city cops. *Stop and listen. Stop your car and listen.* Jim realized it was so simple, almost too simple. He stopped his truck, turning the engine off, leaning out his window.

In the distance, he could hear the distinctive sounds of a car struggling to extract itself from what was probably a hole from the whirling sound its tires were making. Jim knew the sound was close-by due to him hearing a few choice curse words being thrown about.

He was close—real close by the sound of the cars struggle. Jim decided it would be best to pursue on foot the rest of the way. He could have the element of surprise on the suspect. He removed his trusty 38 from the seat beside him, sticking it into his pants waistband before exiting the truck.

The whirling noise had stopped. Evidently the driver had given up. *Good, they would both be on foot.* Jim quickened his pace, staying to the side of the road, seeking some type of security in the massive pine trees that lined both sides of the road.

As he came around a bend, the road opened up. The further he walked, the wider the road seemed to become. After walking around yet another bend, it opened up to reveal an immense lake. Now he realized why the sound of the car was so close. The car lay only 100 yards in front of him parked along the water's edge; its driver's side door tossed wide open, its rear tire evidently still stuck in the mud and the car leaning to one side. *Just as I suspected.*

Jim deliberately advanced to within fifty feet of the car. The lake was now off to his right as he scanned the woods for any sign of the suspect before pressing forward. Jim proceeded towards the suspect's car, weapon facing the front, held securely by both hands in typical police fashion, as he closed the remaining distance to the car's rear.

Jim crouched behind the car knowing full well that the cars aluminum frame wouldn't stand much of a chance stopping a bullet, only hindering its forward progress. He decided the best course of action would be to charge the passenger side door—firing as he went.

Jim had a fully loaded weapon plus a few spare bullets in his pocket if necessary. No time to return to town and drag the local police into this mess. It was up to him.

This would be his first chance to fire his weapon in the line of duty. *Ten years and he never had to fire his weapon.*

Jim started his count down, mentally preparing himself for the suspect to return fire: three, two ....

Peter knew it wouldn't take long until the man realized his rookie mistake and doubled back to the dirt road. This is precisely what Peter had hoped would happen. The difference of a few precious minutes could make or break his plan. This allowed him ample time to spring a simple trap on the unsuspecting police officer; or maybe he was FBI?

From the relative safety of his position in the tree line, Peter could see his prey standing no more than ten meters in front of him. The man appeared ready to charge the vehicle. Exactly what Peter expected, the gung-ho American cowboy type of officer who would not wait for backup. *What a fool!* Peter purposely left his driver's side door ajar to raise some suspicion in the officer's mind. This would be enough to distract him and possibly expend some of his ammunition, leaving him with less to fight with.

Peter held the 9mm firmly in his hands, secretly wishing for a silencer to cap the noise when he fired. You never know if a hunter or hiker would happen upon the scene. Then again, it really didn't matter because the agent would probably fire his weapon when charging his abandoned vehicle.

Peter leaned against one of the abundant pine trees, using one of its branches that happened to be positioned chest high to support for his weapon. Looking through the guns sight, he realized he could shoot him dead from where he stood. But then again, the chance existed that he could also miss or wound him giving away his position and enabling the officer to return fire.

He would allow Allah to choose the moment.

Jim sprung up from behind the car, running to the passenger side where he promptly shot three bullets into the cars empty backseat. Satisfied, he moved on to the front seat and emptied his weapon into what appeared to be a body wrapped in a blanket lying across the seat.

The whole event transpired in a matter of seconds.

Jim held his now empty weapon in the prone position before leaning into the car, closely peering at the blanket. Not wanting to take any chances, he kicked the heavy woolen blanket off what looked to be a body, only to have it reveal six, large tree logs underneath.

Jim stepped away from the car. The suspect was probably watching him right now. He reached for additional bullets in his pocket, able to locate three amongst his change. He ejected the spent cartridges only to hear a twig snap somewhere to the left of him. He turned slowly only to see his prey emerge from the forest.

Jim was now the hunted. Peter the hunter. Peter held his 9mm Beretta in his right hand as he pointed the weapon at Jim's head while using his left hand to signal for Jim to toss his weapon to the ground.

Jim waited several tense seconds before complying, dropping the weapon to the soft earth below.

"My compliments," Peter said. He circled Jim as if a wolf circles its prey. "You stayed with me for a decent amount of time up to this point. You have provided me with some excitement to an otherwise boring drive." He smiled at Jim's predicament then pointed over to the water then back to the forested area. "I must say it is a beautiful country you have here. Unfortunately, I cannot allow you to live and enjoy it any longer. You have stumbled upon something that does not concern you, and you will have to pay for it with your life."

"Somehow I knew you would say that," Jim replied. He watched Peter, waiting for just the right moment to strike. He wasn't going to die without putting up a fight.

"Which department do you work for? FBI? CIA?"

Jim shook his head in response. "Neither one. How about three for a dollar? You can have one more guess."

"You Americans and your wit. Even when facing certain death. I like that." He resumed his pace in front of Jim.

"Let me see, after the FBI and CIA you only have local and state police officials, I take it you are affiliated with one of these agencies?"

"The one and only Atlantic City Police Department at your service," Jim responded, bowing slightly for effect.

Peter could sense that Jim was probing for a weakness in his movement, looking for a way to free himself from his unfortunate situation. With him being employed as an officer of the law, he was surely trained in ways to forcefully take down an armed suspect. Peter decided not to push the prospect, moving back several feet.

"Did you appreciate my little trick with the logs?" Peter pointed to the logs on the front seat. "I learned it the hard way, fighting the Russian troops in my country." He searched Jim's face for any sign of an understanding, sensing none.

"Don't feel bad, you were not the first to fall for such a dastardly trick and you surely will not be the last. I had the pleasure of killing six Russian soldiers with a single hand grenade after they too had searched my car back in Chechnya."

"Chechnya?" Jim said, spitting out his response, a puzzled expression crossing his face. "What in the hell are you doing over here?"

"I am but a simple tourist," Peter replied, once again smiling at Jim. "I am checking out your historical areas before they disappear."

"Come on, you can do better than that. Since you are going to kill me, would you grant me one last request and allow me to ask what you are doing in this country."

"The equivalent of one last cigarette before you die, yes?" Peter said. Usually when his men captured a Russian soldier back in Chechnya they would cut his head off with-in seconds of his surrender, not caring to carry on a conversation with an infidel. The Americans were a different breed, but like their Russian counterparts, infidels just the same.

"Since I don't smoke, I guess you could say that," Jim said. He needed Peter to move just close enough where he could lunge for his weapon. That would be his only chance.

Peter stopped his pacing. He fixed an all-knowing stare at Jim, realizing the man was stalling for time. *If the situation were reversed, I would probably do the same.* "Alright you will have your precious information before you die. But first, I also have a demand to be met. You will have to lay on your stomach. I don't want you to try something silly."

Jim pondered the request for a moment, wondering if he should strike then and there. Knowing that if he were to comply with Peters demand and lay on the ground, he would lose what might be his only chance to overpower the man. He would in effect be signing his own death warrant. No, it had to be now or never. His life was in the balance.

As he stood wondering what action to take, images of his departed wife and son suddenly appeared to him. They looked real enough to reach out and touch. The images stood on the edge of the tree line no more than 15 feet away. Jim smiled as he saw the image of his young son as he stood with a fishing pole two sizes bigger than he was, trying to act cool for an eight year old. Beside his son stood his wife with two suitcases on either side of her, looking impatiently at her watch. It was if they were both waiting for their vacation to start, evidently the one they never had a chance to go on years before, only now *he* was the one holding things up.

Jim eyed Peter as he now stood only five feet away, gun pointed at his head waiting for the right moment to present itself and strike out. Every second that ticked by was a second of his life lost forever. Jim looked past Peter, glancing at the images of his family for reassurance, still waiting, his wife now waving what appeared to be three plane tickets in front of her. She looked radiant in her blue dress he gave her the Christmas before she died. Jim smiled as she pointed to her watch.

Peter glanced to his left wondering what, if anything was behind him. "What are you looking at my friend? Are some more agents closing in behind me that I should know about?"

This was the moment he was looking for.

Jim brought his right leg up in a karate split, kicking the 9mm from Peter's hand, the weapon landing some 10 feet away.

After the initial shock wore off, Peter countered with a quick, one-two blow to Jim's face, pushing him back into the side of Peter's car.

Peter dove for his weapon with Jim following in quick pursuit, him falling on top of Peter as they both struggled for control of the weapon. After several seconds, it wound up in Peter's hand, but not in his control.

Peter seemed the stronger of the two, having just completed his intense physical training in Syria, but Jim was not about to give up, rolling about on the soft ground in a life or death struggle for control of the weapon. They struggled to the water's edge, still rolling and trying to gain control of the weapon. A shot rang harmlessly from the weapons barrel, surprising them both as they stopped struggling for a split moment wondering if the other had been hit. Seeing neither was affected, they resumed their battle. Jim was able to get his finger on the trigger, but Peter still controlled the weapon with his firm grip. Peter once again was able to strike Jim in the face as the struggle ensued, causing the blood from his previous wound to temporarily blind Jim in one eye. When Jim took a moment to wipe away the blood from his eye, Peter escaped his one-armed grasp and jumped up to stand over him, weapon pointed at Jim.

Jim lay on the ground, struggling to search for his families apparitions in the tree line, panicking when they vanished, only to reappear beside him, one on each side, ready to help him to his feet.

"Goodbye, American," Peter said, backing up several feet to avoid any blood splatter on his clothing, the bullet entering the center of Jim's chest, killing him instantly.

Peter quickly searched Jim's pockets for his truck keys, thinking it would be best to take his vehicle and throw *the proverbial dogs off the scent*.

Jim's body lay on the water's edge. Nothing could have saved him that day. The shot went right through his heart. It took only seconds for his life to drain away.

It would be another senseless killing, one whose numbers would only increase by day's end, *possibly by a million fold*.

Reaching the end of the fire road where it intersected with the macadam highway, Peter turned left announcing his intention of driving to Washington. He had only hours to reach Washington DC and keep his strict timetable.

Jim opened his eyes several minutes after the initial gun blast, remembering the feel of the hot lead as it ripped into his chest. He blinked his eyes several times in response to the suns intense rays wondering what the hell had happened. More than that, *where was he?* Looking from side-to-side, he couldn't help but notice the vivid colors of the leaves; they seemed brighter, clearer. The hues were magnificent. *What the hell was going on?*

From his position on the ground, he saw a dark wavy figure running down the road he had just traveled. *Was that the man who just shot me?*

A sudden rush of warmth enveloped his body feeling as though he had stepped into a bubbling hot tub. *This is crazy,* blinking several times as if it would help in answering his questions.

Looking down at his shirt, he saw that there was neither blood nor a gunshot hole. *What the.....? I know I was shot. I didn't just dream the whole thing up. It was too intense of a feeling.* Jim struggled to his feet. Blinking several times, feeling as if he were a newborn to this world, Jim looked around to see the suspect's car. *It actually did happen!* He saw his 38 caliber on the ground.

Jim felt the hairs on the back of his neck stand tall when he heard the unmistakable laugh of a child ring out. He saw his son fishing in the shallow bank of the lake pulling a 3-pound rainbow trout from its depths, holding it high in order to gauge its length.

That's my son! He wanted to say aloud, but an uncontrollable force was stopping him from speaking.

Unbeknownst to Jim, his wife had silently laid a picnic basket on a blanket beside where he now stood. She was trying to smooth the winkles in her blue dress, trying to look her best for the man she had fell madly in love with at fifteen years of age. She stood looking at him, noticing that he hadn't changed a bit except for a few extra pounds around the waist.

Laura decided not to say anything, clearing her throat in order to get his attention. Jim turned in response and was now face to face with his true love. She stood smiling coyly in front of him.

But this can't be real, he thought. If it were possible, she was even more beautiful than he had remembered. He was dumfounded, wanting to say something but she quickly applied a manicured finger to his lips.

"Welcome home!" Laura whispered lovingly, following it up with a passionate kiss. She then pulled out a clip that held her hair in place, shaking her head from side-to-side, allowing her long hair to fall freely about her.

"Yes, I remembered that you hated my hair *scrunched up in a ball*." Her throaty laugh resonating through the area's pine trees. She stood there for him to admire in all her splendor, spinning around in her blue dress as the wind lifted it up slightly as she twirled it back and forth. Jim wondered if this were all a dream and he would suddenly find himself awake and back in his dreary apartment in Atlantic City.

Laura suddenly raised her hand to her lips, causing Jim to look down at himself as if he were to blame. "My goodness, how foolish of me, I almost forgot," she said, quickly turning towards a figure standing alone in the shallow waters of the lake. "Bobby, come over here. Your father's home," she said, reaching out to take his hand in hers. Laura smiled once more at him, repeating the word, *"home"* admiring its sound as if hearing it for the first time.

Up to this point Bobby had been unaware of his father's presence amongst them, still busy trying to gauge his fish's size. No longer, Jim could see his son dropping his fishing pole and freshly caught fish in the water in response to his mother's message, bounding through the lakes shallow waters as if running the high hurdles to join them in their joyful reunion.

Yes, he was surely home.

CHAPTER SIXTEEN

Ocean City, New Jersey

Alice looked at the note and nodded, "Thanks, sergeant, I'll give this to my supervisor." She abruptly closed the door behind her, walking back down the steps to where Michael Forsythe was still interrogating Boris.

"Michael, can I see you for a minute?" She motioned him over to an isolated part of the holding area, out of earshot of Boris.

"What do we have Alice?"

Alice handed him the note.

"So, we have our man heading west do we? Well, I guess we can tell our Russian friend here the good news," turning back to face Boris. "We have located your friend running west, probably heading towards Washington or south to Norfolk. Which one is it Boris? Is he returning to your old stomping grounds in DC?"

Alice leaned over to Forsythe, whispering in his ear about the Washington and Philadelphia maps that were found in the suspect's car.

"Forsythe clapped his hands together. "Boris, the pieces of the puzzle keep coming together, even without your help." He walked back over to where Boris sat handcuffed to the metal chair.

Boris looked tired. The exertion, both mental and physical, had taken its toll. He struggled to hold up his head. "I still don't know what you are talking about, Michael. I am but a simple Russian citizen who has come to vacation at your lovely beaches. Since my arrival, I have been insulted and assaulted by your police."

Forsythe delivered yet another nasty blow to the face, opening up a second cut below his right eye. "Cut the crap, Boris. Answer truthfully to the next question or so help me, I'll pummel you senseless. You and your accomplice will not harm any of our citizens, not on my watch. I swear on my mother's grave it will not happen. If I kill you here, we can save the American taxpayer a lot of money. Answer the damn question."

Boris realized Michael was serious. His face beet red, eyes bulging, and he honestly believed he would kill him if provided the chance. The time for a deal never quite surfaced, thinking it was out of the question. It was time for Boris to save what he could and the hell with the young Muslim. Boris tried to salvage some dignity, sitting up straight, wiping the blood from his face.

"All right, Michael, you win. I will answer your questions as truthfully and honestly as I can."

Forsythe had to be restrained by his fellow agents.

"That's the same shit you said hours ago Boris and look where we are!" he screamed.

Boris chalked one up for himself, one of the few he could attest too. He was able to upset the esteemed, Michael

Forsythe, just enough for him to lose his sense of judgment in front of his subordinates. Known in his FSB dossier as a cool customer, that notion would be updated to reflect today's actions. The game tilted in Boris's favor, but not for long. He had to start feeding Michael some relevant information, or he might pay dearly, possibly with his life.

Boris nodded his thanks to each agent for saving him from yet another beating.

"Michael, the man I agreed to meet down here is an agent for the Chechnya government," Boris stating the first factual bit of information after three hours of harsh interrogation.

Forsythe took his time wiping blood from Boris's face with a handkerchief. "Okay, Boris, let's start fresh," he said in a barely audible tone. "The man you met with on the Ocean City Boardwalk, who did he work for? What is his name?" He motioned for one of his fellow agents to release the handcuffs as a sign of good will.

"Like I said before Michael, the man works for the Chechnya government. He is a rebel freedom fighter, recruited to become an agent of his government." Boris paused and then held a handkerchief to the cut above his eye to stem the flow of blood.

He continued. "From what I have heard through my sources, he went to Syria to train for a mission to be executed in the United States. He is now operating under the alias of a Peter Zar..... something or another. I can't remember the rest of his name."

Forsythe had a gut feeling that Boris was ready to spill everything. His back was to the wall, and he knew it.

Boris struggled to look at his watch, blood still trickling down, obscuring his vision; he brought his Platinum Rolex up to several inches from his right eye. "I can feed you one juicy tidbit of information," he said, looking around at his captor's as they awaited his next disclosure. *Boris loved to play the game of chess since mastering the game at a young age and this would be a masterful move, enabling him to extract a "Draw" from a situation only minutes before was a "Checkmate."*

"You will have to pardon me Michael, my eyes are not what they used to be," he said, allowing the agents in the room to emit a brief chuckle considering the situation. "For this bit of information you will allow me to continue to New York to catch a Swiss Air flight to Geneva. I promise you that after you hear my information, I will be the least bit of your worries."

Forsythe smiled at Alice, shaking his head at what hours of interrogation could yield. "I will promise you this much, Boris; if the information you provide is substantial and I mean *substantial*, I will take your terms under advisement. I might even consider flying you to New York myself if it's juicy enough!"

It was Boris' turn to smile about the room for he was about to take his opponent's queen and end the game. "Michael, may I bother you for a glass of water," pointing to the pitcher on the table in the center of the room. "I'm a bit parched from all of this heat."

He watched as Alice obliged and filled the glass, handing it to him.

He downed the content in one swift tilt of the glass, his first drink since they had started the beatings.

"Michael, I would suggest you warm up your jet for me," looking from agent to agent in order to build up the suspense, convinced he held their rapt attention before continuing.

"In approximately five hours, one of your American cities will lose its entire downtown area in a small nuclear explosion."

Checkmate.

CHAPTER SEVENTEEN

Moscow, Russia

General Poszk relaxed in the plush surroundings of his Ministry office. He sat re-reading the interrogation proceedings for Sirna. *If the rest of the Chechnya rebel leadership is made of the same material as this man, God help us.*

A soft knock at his office door caused him to close the file, placing it in his desk drawer.

Looking up, he saw his secretary, a matronly woman of 70. "General, you have a Captain Igor Isinov to see you," she said.

"Show him in please," he responded. The general stood up from behind his desk and walked over to a table filled with various liquors from his worldly travels. Standing before his table, he focused in on a bottle of Jim Beam, an American

Bourbon he had picked up a taste for while working as a Military Attaché at the Russian Embassy in Washington DC. General Poszk contemplated ordering something to eat from his secretary, but thought better of it. The torture session he had witnessed earlier upset his stomach. He needed a good stiff drink. The drink would also settle his nerves since reading the red presidential folder on his desk, a gift from one of his intelligence friends in the FSB.

Captain Isinov stepped into the general's office in his dress uniform, proudly displaying his ribbons or "fruit salad" on his chest. The rows of ribbons attested to his many combat actions in Afghanistan, Angola, Chechnya and advisor ships in Syria, Libya, and Vietnam.

"Captain Isinov reporting as ordered sir," he said, executing a crisp salute.

The general held up a bottle of Jim Beam in return salute. "Relax captain, we can be informal here. What can I get for you? Swedish vodka? Canadian whiskey? You pick your poison as the Americans say and I will find it for you." He extended his open hand over the motley collection of bottles he had amassed as gifts in his travels.

"Nothing for me sir, I am still on duty," Captain Isinov replied, still standing at attention with his body ramrod straight.

General Poszk shook his head in response. "Captain, at ease! That is an order! If you keep up these military shenanigans, I will court martial you right here. Now relax, you have a long journey in front of you. Under the current situation, I think a stiff belt would ease your burdens." He picked up a Czechoslovakian crystal tumbler and filled it halfway with his own personal choice of Jim Beam, dropping in two ice cubes. "I have made the selection for you captain. I know how you prefer a good French wine when you can get a hold of it, but this will have to do for now. For the moment, please sit down and try some of this outstanding American bourbon while we discuss your mission."

Captain Isinov relaxed, thanking the general for his generosity. Such a drink would cost him a day's wages if he ordered it in a bar.

The general picked up the folder with a red presidential seal across its front, the word "Top Secret" marked at its top. "It will only take you a few minutes, read this document and tell me what you think."

"But general, I am not cleared to this level."

General Poszk leaned over his desk in encouragement and slid the now open folder in front of the captain. "There, it is open, captain. You have my permission to read the document. Jesus Christ, Igor, we have been friends for a long time now. I would not allow harm to come to you. You have my word on it."

Not wanting to offend the general any further, he started to read the single-spaced, two page document.

To the general's amusement, he reread the document as if not believing or wanting to believe what he had said. After the second reading, the captain picked up his glass of bourbon and finished its contents in one gulp.

"That's a precious commodity captain savor it!" the general said, knowing full well that he had the same reaction when he first read the document.

"General, this is no joke? I mean the words in this folder are all true?"

The general nodded. "When our prisoner Sirna Miliruid alluded to weapons of mass destruction, it was to be no joke. You were in the room, you heard him say those words. After Sirna's disclosure, I inquired at the very top about the possibilities of such weapons being compromised, *or hell*, even existing. When I informed our President of the prisoner's recent boasting, his eyes went wide. Igor, when I say wide, I mean he was scared. *Really scared*. After our meeting, he handed me the folder you have just read." The general paused, looking him straight in the eye before continuing. "So you can see Igor, Sirna told us the truth."

The captain sat back in his chair, wondering who had ever envisioned such a nightmare scenario in the first place. "You mean we actually placed nuclear weapons in the United States? This is no joke?"

The general nodded once more.

"General, if the Americans know about this, they most likely have implemented the same strategy to use against us. They would be fools not too. And we both know they are not fools."

The bourbon in his glass finished, the general reached for a pack of cigarettes. He extracted one before offering the same to the captain.

The captain stopped smoking weeks before but now he needed one more than ever.

"You are correct in your assumption captain," the general said, lighting the captain's cigarette, then his own. "We have firsthand knowledge that the Americans planted roughly the same amount of "suitcase weapons" that we planted in their country. So, they have effectively evened the playing field.

The captain exhaled his smoke into the air above him. "God help us all. Anyone could strike and kill the other before they had any chance of possibly responding."

"Now you know the reason for the plan's implementation. The other would not dare strike, knowing what would happen in response. A first strike was no longer deemed an option, its risk too great to exercise." He paused to look at photos of his grandchildren, wondering what type of life they would have if this lunatic were to succeed in his mission. "That is exactly why you and you alone are heading to the United States. Your mission when you arrive, to hunt down this rebel before he starts World War Three. Starting from this minute on, you will have less than 64 hours before this rebel is to strike. We know the rebel's first target will be in Washington DC."

"General, we could insert a small team of specialists around the Washington location and await our rebel to show and then eliminate the bastard? That way our weapons could stay put in their present locations and the adversary is dead. We could have the best of both situations without it affecting us."

General Poszk pondered the captain's response for several seconds. He rose from his desk, extinguishing his cigarette in an ashtray, and walked back over to his where his bottle of Jim Beam lay. "Captain, what I have said to you and what I am about to tell you stays in this office, Top Secret. Not even your wife is to know of our discussion. Is that understood?"

"I understand fully sir," the captain replied.

General Poszk poured himself another generous drink, in the process not offering to refill the captains. He had already shared enough of his private stock and Christmas was still four months off.

"We have a problem with our weapons location," taking a sip of his drink before he proceeded. "According to our sources, the two weapons are just the beginning. We evidently have thirty more whose locations may already have been compromised. We apparently had a mole in our Washington DC office who has come back to roost. Now you know our larger problem. As for your suggestion to eliminate him, a team of specialists would draw attention to our little problem. We know that the American National Security Agency has monitored all of our coded telephone transactions, and it is only a matter of time before their master cryptologists break it. And they will eventually break it, Igor; the Americans are very good at what they do. You may ask, how do we perform damage control on our end? From what we understand, the first one is definitely in the open. So it is only a matter of time until it's removed or," pausing as he finished the contents of his glass, "*detonated.*"

Captain Isinov sat staring at the general for several seconds, mesmerized by the last statement, focusing on the word *detonated*. "What exactly do you expect of me general?"

The general turned to his young counterpart, admiring his courage, knowing why he had selected him and him alone for this urgent mission. He had a short list of names he could trust to accomplish the mission. Only the captain's name stood out.

"You, my friend are to fly to Washington DC aboard a Delta Airlines flight that departs in two hours. Once in Washington, you will head to the location we have provided you and remove the weapon under the cover of darkness. Use your own ingenuity to remove it, I am told it cannot explode without the proper codes. You will then call this number at the embassy," he handed him a standard white business card with a telephone number, "and you will receive further instructions. It is important that you do not mention anything about the weapon to this man over the phone lines; only recite these numbers below the telephone number. You will then proceed with the weapon to a payphone located one block from the Embassy. You will once again call the embassy and recite the second set of numbers below the first. No need to worry about the remaining weapons, they will be collected over the next three months by special teams and returned before something like this could happen again. Right now, we are only concerned with the disclosed weapon. As for the rebel, we will allow the American FBI to deal with him," smirking as he said it. "We will disclose to the Americans that we have a renegade spy who is in their midst with a death wish. He is an Islamic fundamentalist who seeks revenge for their harsh treatment of Afghanistan. That should have him quickly disposed of."

General Poszk handed a white paper airline ticket with Delta written in bold red lettering across its face to the captain. "You will be completely on your own until you contact the embassy. Up until that time, you are considered somewhat of a renegade yourself. I think you understand why it must be this way? We are walking on new ground with the Americans, actually helping our former enemy hunt down terrorists like this one who is operating in the United States."

The general handed him a glass capsule the size of an ordinary cold tablet. "Just in case you get caught. Don't worry, from what I hear from our folks in the FSB department, the capsule works within five seconds of biting down. They also inform me, it is painless."

Captain Isinov understood the consequences of mission failure and nodded solemnly before biding a quick exit.

CHAPTER EIGHTEEN

In the skies above Southern Chechnya

The black dot was barely visible to the naked eye, and even if it were to be noticed, would present no issue to those viewing it from below. Many high-flying passenger jets still utilized the skies above, flying at distances well above the older model Surface to Air Missile's range that the Chechnya rebels stored in their inventory.

In the skies above, Lieutenant Georgy Rogonivich expertly maneuvered his lumbering Blackjack Bomber. With his target now approaching, he pulled back the throttles on the center console, slowing the massive aircraft from 1,100 knots to just under 400. With beautiful weather presenting itself at 5,000 meters above the Nakyata Pass, he adhered to his navigator's strict demands to steer a course of 170 degrees. This enabled him to follow the narrow outline of the deep canyon below.

"Remember Sergi, we are looking to drop this stuff on the rams head portion of the canyon," Georgy said to his young bombardier, a Second Lieutenant straight out of the Military Academy.

"We could end this rebellion with one click of your well trained thumb," looking back to gauge his response.

Georgy could see from the boy's expression that he could not take a joke.

"Don't worry, we have 30 of those 1,000 kilo bad boys in our bomb bay, you only have to hit them with one," laughing out loud at the second lieutenant's expression of panic.

"Target, two miles ahead, Rams Head positively identified below," the navigator said in a voice resembling a teenager on the verge of puberty. "Opening the bomb bay doors and I am taking command of the aircraft, Lieutenant."

"Affirmative," Georgy said in reply, the humor now gone. It was down to business.

Omar Turhaniz moved about his headquarters compound with the swiftness of a rabbit. At times, he seemed to be in multiple places at once, from directing the clerks and secretary's to overseeing the security forces. Omar knew he had to inspire his charges to move quickly and leave nothing behind for the Russians to use. This meant destroying anything that was not transportable, including the water supply and latrine facilities.

Their only means of air defense, an antiquated radar system donated by the Iranian military, was shut down 30 minutes earlier. After the radar unit, its accompanying SAM-8 battery, another gift of the Iranians, was disassembled for travel. This left the Headquarters area defenseless from an air attack. Omar did strategically position five observers with high-power binoculars on the surrounding cliffs to scan all approaches, both ground and air.

Since moving to this site from their previous headquarters three years before, the Russian Military had been totally inept at locating them. With only one or two hours remaining, that record would seem to remain intact.

With an infection to his right foot hindering his progress, Omar limped from truck-to-truck. He busily instructed the drivers on what routes they would follow to the new headquarters in the Goltea caves. Even though they would operate at night, in a convoy, the possibility did present itself that they could come under attack along the way.

Omar wouldn't allow one truck nor one body to be left for the Russians. He instructed his men to wire all of the trucks with demolition charges in case they encountered the enemy. The two pounds of Semtex each truck carried would effectively obliterate any trace of the trucks and its cargo.

Most of the work had been mundane; consisting of packing everything from cots for sleeping to foodstuffs. Omar stood proudly surveying the area that his staff had broken down in a remarkable four days. They were now in the process of loading into the last of the 10 Mazda trucks for their short, but treacherous journey.

Omar waved to the last truck driver, limping over to shake his hand.

Omar never reached the truck as a sudden shrill sounded from above, the earth around him shook violently in a massive series of explosions. Omar first saw the lead truck and his 3rd in command disappear via a huge fireball, the explosions rumbling towards his position consuming truck after truck and the earth surrounding them. Omar turned to run from the convoy and hopefully to safety when struck by a cluster bomb fragment from behind. He quickly succumbed to injuries before yet another bomb shredded apart his body as if it were paper.

It was a quick and painless death for him, unlike the many Russian soldiers and airmen he had murdered.

The resulting explosions engulfed the entire complex area for a kilometer in radius, dismembering most of the rebel's bodies into hundreds of small fragments.

There was nothing left to bury, only DNA to be examined.

CHAPTER NINETEEN

Heathrow International Airport - London, England

The Delta flight from Moscow touched down at London's Heathrow airport, arriving in time for its passengers to enjoy a full English breakfast. Igor enjoyed the comfort provided by traveling on a civilian airline versus a military transport; at least he knew they would not end up in a potential hostile environment upon landing.

Before leaving Moscow, General Poszk had pulled Igor aside and informed him that the Captain had an appointment to call on Sir Robert John, Director of MI-6, and to relay the complete story to him. *In effect, putting all of their cards on the table.*

Igor hoped Sir Robert would take pity on a wary traveler and send a car for him instead of forcing him to take the damn train. With only a three-hour layover in London, he figured wasting at least two hours in traveling, one in each direction. The last time he visited London, he wound up getting lost taking the subway or *the Tube* as the Brits endearingly referred to it—winding up back at the airport dazed and confused—finally deciding to take a Taxi to his hotel. *Hopefully the urgency of the situation would command VIP treatment* Igor thought as he picked up his single leather garment bag from the baggage carousel, preparing for immigration inspection.

Sir Robert John and General Poszk had history together, with both having served their governments in Germany, West and East, during the turbulent 70's and early 80's. One essentially spying on the other. After 30 years in the business, they each had reached the pinnacle of their government service. Over time, they developed a mutual admiration for each other, even golfing together once a year to increase détente.

Igor's mission would only solidify their informal partnership.

He felt uneasy standing in the passport control line, forced to travel incognito and using his civilian attire. It may seem absurd to some civilian, but there was something about the wearing of a uniform that provided a sense of security; a feeling of belonging. Standing in the long line of many nationalities made him feel, *naked.*

Igor stood behind a large, middle-aged group of vacationers from Kiev, knowing that the overhead security cameras had been focused on each of them from the time they left the aircraft. Their pictures would be run through an existing database containing thousands of pictures of known intelligence agents or terrorists. A giant leap in technology from the 70's or 80's when each airport control would have five to ten security agents watching the disembarking passengers to compare black and white photos of known terrorists or foreign agents. The airports would purposely stall the passengers by making them wait 45 minutes for their luggage to show on the carousal then an hour for passport control. This provided time for the security personnel to manually compare each passenger to the photos. That was in the past, as archaic as radial engines on aircraft for passenger travel. The new computers at Heathrow would digitally scan each unsuspecting disembarking passenger and electronically send each image to its massive database, comparing the picture took mere seconds for the hi-power TROLIC software. When the software did find a match it spat out the results to a waiting team of security agents who would indiscreetly "assist" the subject in question to an interrogation suite.

Igor noticed that a well-dressed couple had suddenly staked out a position beside him. Igor nodded to the woman, a well-built red head wearing an expensively tailored business suit. She in turn, shot him a quick all knowing glance, sizing him up from head to toe. Igor then looked to the man, taking note of his impeccably tailored Seville Row pinstriped suit and handcrafted leather briefcase. The briefcase was one that he carried strangely with both hands, the case in front of his chest. Funny, he hadn't noticed the smartly dressed couple on his Delta flight. *He would have undoubtedly noticed the red head.*

The redhead leaned into Igor causing him to instinctively reach for his wallet having heard horror stories about pickpockets operating throughout the airport complex.

She produced a badge for him alone to see. "We work for MI-5, Captain Isinov," she whispered softly into his ear.

"Police matter. Would you please not make a scene and follow us." She pointed to the man in the pin stripped suit now stationed to his left, producing a 9mm weapon from behind the leather briefcase. "We would like a few words with you," she said in an impeccable, upper class accent.

The man in the pin stripe suit walked toward a door that had only seconds before contained a wall of two-way mirrors.

Igor had a distinctive feeling that the facial recognition software was up and running.

"Please come in and have a seat, sir," the man in the pin stripped suit said, allowing the red head to close the door behind them.

"We've been waiting for you," the red head said. She carefully removed Igor's bag from his shoulder.

He was about to protest. But how could he? With him outnumbered two to one in a foreign country.

"What are you doing in Great Britain, sir?" The agent in the pin stripped suit said, studying Igor's body movements for any tell tale signs.

"I am here for an appointment with the Director of MI-6, Sir Robert John," Igor stated, knowing it would probably sound like some type of joke to these agents. "If I'm not mistaken, isn't his organization ranked somewhat higher than your MI-5 with you representing internal security, and him on a more national scale?"

The red head was already searching his garment bag with her skillful fingers, moving them carefully over his bags seams before locating the false compartment in its bottom.

"What, no appointment with the Queen?" she replied in jest.

"It's no joke, miss. Call him yourself. I have his personal number in my bag," Igor replied gruffly.

The redhead looked over to her counterpart, a smug look on her face. "Captain, why do you have a false panel in the bottom of your bag? And why," holding up his pistol for the agent in the pinstripe suit to see, "does it contain a weapon?"

Igor smiled in response, wondering how long it would take a professional to locate his weapon. "I am, as you British say, on the clock, working a job."

Still studying his bag, the redhead was able to come up with yet another false compartment, this one containing a 1/2-kilogram of Semtex and its accompanying detonator. "Jesus, Mary, and Joseph, she said aloud. "And what the hell were you planning to do with this?" She gently placed the explosive clay on the table for display. "Call in some help, I want this man strip searched, X-rayed and then arrested."

"Damn it," Igor exclaimed. "Sir Robert is expecting me. You have to believe me. Call him yourself. His personal number is on a piece of paper in the false compartment. Just take the time and look would you!" The frustration was clearly evident in his voice.

No sooner had Igor finished pleading his case when the inner door leading from the opposite hallway opened, revealing a slender, middle-aged man, attired in a worn plaid sport coat and accompanying slacks. The smell of pipe smoke entered with him. He had a genuine look of authority about him as he straightened his Royal Guards tie.

The man in the pin stripe suit quickly pulled out his standard issue 9mm, pointing it at the new visitor. "Who the hell are you, Mate? Identify yourself and be quick about it," wondering how he had evaded the guard stationed outside the room.

The man in the sport coat reached slowly for his inside coat pocket, stopping as the agent in the pin stripe suit proceeded to complete his movement for him, extracting his government issued identification.

"Let's see who we have here shall we," the agent in the pinstripe suit said before cursing under his breath, returning the gold embossed identification. "Sir Robert, I'm terribly sorry for the inconvenience. I apologize for not recognizing you, sir.
"

Sir Robert John nodded curtly to both agents. "No harm, you were only doing your job now weren't you? If you could be so kind and please leave myself and the captain alone to discuss some items of national security, it would be greatly appreciated."

The agent with the red hair pointed to the weapon and the block of Semtex. "Wait a minute, Sir Robert. What about this stuff on the table? No matter who you are, we can't let this come into the country." She stubbornly stood her ground against England's most powerful spymaster.

Sir Robert admired her for her perseverance. He removed his cell phone and dialed the head of MI-5. "Byron, its Sir Robert here. One of your people is having a hard time understanding the situation. Would you be so kind as to inform her of the ground rules?"

Sir Robert handed his phone to the attractive agent.

The agent listened in silence as the Director of MI-5 read her the riot act. After several minutes of an uncomfortable silence, she set the phone down in front of Sir Robert, nodding her thanks for its use.

She searched for the right words as she stood in front of Sir Robert, wondering if her career would be affected by her overzealous attitude. "I must apologize for my actions, Sir Robert, this is your show. I was unaware up to this point. Please don't hold my actions against the security service I work for, it's not their fault."

Sir Robert raised his hands in order to cut her off. "You were only doing your job. I must commend you on your actions. Now, good day to you both."

Sir Robert ignored his seated guest for the moment, choosing to concentrate on his leather briefcase, removing a red folder with "Eye's Only" emblazoned across its front in bold black lettering.

"Pardon me for being so rude," said Sir Robert before reaching across the table to shake his hand. "Captain Igor Isinov, so nice to finally meet you."

Igor was surprised at the strength of the older man's grip.

"I have heard many good things about you from General Poszk. The General says you are his proverbial *ace in the hole* when it comes to operations such as we have here," he pointed to the folder that lay in front of him. "Do you have any idea why General Poszk asked you to see me during your layover in London?"

Igor sat casually looking about the room, bracing himself for the unexpected. "No sir, but I am sure you will be informing me of something very interesting and soon." He allowed a slight smile to escape. *"It's been that type of day."*

Sir Robert could see they would get along famously, admiring his levity for the moment. "You are correct, Captain," suppressing his own need to smile as he rose from the table. "General Poszk has many enemies in his own government," walking over to inspect a tourism poster for the upcoming Shakespeare Festival in Stratford-upon-Avon. "He could not trust the information to be spoken on Russian soil," turning back around to face Igor. "The walls have ears is another way of stating what he could not say. His every move is scrutinized by his enemies internal to your own government; he even told me that both his office and private home are under constant electronic surveillance. Poor chap."

"I was aware the General had enemies but not on so great of a magnitude," Igor replied. He wondered if his own home was bugged due to his close dealings with the general. Igor thought about calling his wife when his meeting with Sir Robert adjourned. That thought quickly dashed due to the possibility of the phone also being bugged.

Sir Robert realized the time was right. He was adhering to General Poszk's strict guidance, one that if he did not immediately concur with the decision to send Captain Isinov to the United States, he could send one of his own people in his place. Having read and then dissected the captain's personnel folder, he concurred with the general's selection. They required a covert soldier and most importantly, according to the general—*a man beyond trustworthy.*

Sir Robert walked back to his leather briefcase, extracting a recent tour guide of Israel, one with a bright color picture of the Temple Mount on its cover. He casually tossed it across to Igor.

"Something is up your sleeve, Sir Robert, and I feel General Poszk has volunteered my services for another type of mission." Igor now wondered what the hell he was getting himself into.

Sir Robert stood at the opposite side of the table, dismissing his comment with a sly grin. "Captain, have you ever been to Israel on holiday or possibly for a work related cause?" Sir Robert knew full well that Russia had numerous spies in the state of Israel, this with the ongoing exodus of Russian emigrants to Israel.

"I never had the pleasure, Sir Robert, but it is on my to-do list when I retire some day."

Sir Robert decided to sit down beside Igor instead of across from him, in effect not preaching down to him. After all, they were now team members. In his line of business, he always tried to intimidate, whether it was politicians nipping away at his budget or surly supervisors trying to unseat him. Not in this case, the Captains exploits and skills spoke volumes about the man and Sir Robert was an excellent judge of character.

"How rude of me, where are my manners. I cannot have you return home and say British hospitality was lacking now could I? Would you like a cup of coffee or another type of beverage perhaps? Maybe a pastry?

"No, thank you, Sir Robert. I'll just take the bad news that you have to provide me, straight up."

Sir Robert looked at Igor and realized why General Poszk placed his trust in the man. He had been forewarned that he was a no bullshit kind of soldier. All of this came clearly across to Sir Robert. "Okay, by now you must be wondering what this is all about?" Sir Robert pointed to the room's surroundings and then to the tour book that lay on the table. "An old soldier such as yourself is probably wondering when the rubber hoses and wooden bats are coming out?"

They both laughed aloud at the prospect, but the harsh reality being that just 20 years earlier that probably would have been the situation. Since the fall of the Soviet Union, everything changed, including cooperation between the two former enemies.

"But enough of the past. General Poszk and I have a proposition for you. *Well, I have a proposition for you.* The general has already ordered you on the mission. It's the alteration to the mission that you might have some contention with. It pertains to something we thought up a few years ago. At the time it was nothing more of *what if* fantasy and a bit of a dream then its chance of ever becoming reality. That was up until this nuclear suitcase issue comes about. Immediately, we both realized the potential of the situation."

Igor nodded.

Sir John continued. "If you agree, you will be going on a short visit to the United States just as previously planned, then on to Israel for us, meaning General Poszk and myself. Upon completion of the Israel portion of the mission, you will retire. You are being forced to retire by the general because he said, and I am quoting him here when I say this," taking a piece of paper from his briefcase and removing his glasses to read the small print. *"'The old bear has done enough for his country, it's time to hibernate,'* unquote. I imagine you have a good idea of what he is referring too?"

Igor nodded once more, realizing the general was trying to protect him due to the political turmoil going on back home. This was his way of saying thank-you and to stay low and away from him.

"Now, if you don't mind, Captain, back to the matter at hand." He cast a uncomfortable gaze his way. "You are going to perform a mission of the utmost secrecy. Nothing higher than this, my boy."

"Sir Robert, I understood the risks before I left Russia. The only thing that has changed is the recent addition of going to Israel. As I first said to General Poszk and now to you, I am willing to die for this mission. That should be enough to calm your fears of my maintaining *mission secrecy*. I think the question should be how are you going to maintain secrecy on your end?"

"Touché, Captain. I admire your jab. To answer your question, I alone will know of this. No one else on the British side, not even the Prime Minister will hear about this until the time is right. Let's dispense with the appetizer and jump right into the main course shall we? The governments of Russia and Great Britain have been secretly negotiating a Middle-East peace settlement with Israel, Jordan, Syria, Egypt, and the Palestinians. We have decided to brush aside the United States and their half-hearted attempts of peace and decided to take a more radical approach to the process."

"Since when does Great Britain and Russia co-operate on a peace treaty? Has Hell frozen over? We in Russia have always thought of the United States and yourself as one nation, one enemy. Only the United States seemed to be your mouthpiece."

Sir Robert understood his animosity, knowing their countries past histories and entanglements. "Yes, some of us in Great Britain are of the same thought. Times change my young Russian friend. We are always looking for new opportunities. When this one presented itself, we jumped at the chance to show the Americans we are still a sovereign nation. We will achieve peace on the first go-around."

"And how do you intend on achieving this peace?"

"It's simplistic in nature. You will go to the United States and perform your mission as originally planned. Find the suitcase weapon and bring it back to us here in London. As for your embassy in Washington, inform them that when you reached the location of the weapon it had already been unearthed. They will obviously blame that rebel chap you are after for its disappearance, and assume it is back in their homeland somewhere. Once back in London, General Poszk, myself, and of course you, will escort the weapon with a combination of MI-6 and General's handpicked team members to Jerusalem. Neither team will be informed of the precious cargo we carry, only yourself. We will inform the others that we are on some sort of joint training exercise or something along those lines.

"Once in Jerusalem we will proceed to the area around the Temple Mount, the holiest shrine for Christians, Muslims and the Jewish people. The Temple Mount holds the significance of all three religions, therefore it commands absolute attention," Sir Robert said. "Stop me if I'm proceeding too fast for you old boy."

The captain simply nodded allowing for him to proceed.

"The weapon will then be buried 10 meters underground in a chamber that the Israelis are presently excavating under the guise of an archeological dig. Again, only the leader of Mossad is aware of the full operation. Even the laborers performing the work have no idea. Presently, only the Israeli's are involved. We haven't let the other countries in on the full operational details yet. Once the initial part of the mission is complete, we will then summon all of the Middle East participants to the peace table, inform them of the buried weapon and then lay *our terms* on the table." Sir Robert sat staring once again at Igor, evidently wondering how he would react to such a radical plan, or a delicious opportunity as they in Whitehall saw it.

Igor sat back for a moment trying to read between the lines of the operation; *there was always something hidden between the lines.* Sitting back in his chair, he had many questions and concerns but thought better, this was neither the time nor the place. He would state the obvious to Sir Robert, and then back away.

"Your plan sounds achievable, but what keeps the Arabs from still attacking Israel?"

Sir Robert leaned back in his chair; it was his turn to smile, anticipating just such a question. "Remember, I said it is simplistic in nature so lower your normal standards of thinking, Captain. Since the Temple Mount is the principle piece holding the religions together, it could also destroy them. When we approach the table, we will inform the Arabs that the weapon is buried in the Temple Mount and set to explode if any attack happens upon Israel. Not a minor shooting or stabbing mind you but a heavy attack or invasion. In one quick motion, we will guarantee security for the region. We then initiate the idea of a Palestinian State but only on the west bank and then saturate the area with United Nations troops on the ground as peacekeepers. The Gaza strip reverts back to Israeli control. The Israeli's have already stated they will accept the idea of a state if we supply the security. Who wants to be the instigator that causes the destruction of the holiest shrine representing three key religions?"

This was clever, thought Igor, wondering who had first proposed such a brilliant idea, Sir John or General Poszk? He thought both men of being capable. "Who is going to hold the activation keys for the weapon?" Igor knew full well from his recent training that the weapon had to be manually keyed in order to achieve detonation. This weapon is to be buried under 10 feet of earth or concrete.

"We will change the configuration of the weapon to enable it to accept an outside source code via a transmitter for it to explode," Sir Robert said. "The transmitter will be held by a responsible panel. The objective will be the same that the old Soviet Union achieved with the United States in the 70's. The Soviet Union stopped the United States from a pre-emptive strike by storing the weapons on United States soil. As you know, once the US found out about the weapons, all first strike scenarios were removed from the US playbook. The US could not strike due to the buried Soviet weapons near military installations and US cities. Their missile silos were for all intent, neutered. We will use the same analogy; you make a move and we destroy something you hold dear and precious. This alone will cause the process to really start in earnest."

Igor decided to press the issue. "Why not just use one of your own weapons from storage, or an Israeli one? Why wait for the suitcase weapon in the United States?" *It made perfect sense, at least to himself. Everyone knows the Israeli's possess the same type of weapons. Why couldn't they just donate one from their stockpile?*

Sir Robert smiled at him. "We would be laughed from the room with that suggestion. And that would be perfectly understandable. But if you have a weapon that is not supposed to exist, like the ones your country placed in the United States, who is going to miss them? Hell, your own government can't even afford to disable or store the ones it has placed in your own country. The weapons in the United States are something they inherited from the previous administration. They have to beg from the United States for monies to pull back the 32 weapons in order to destroy them. Is this an irony of the Cold War?"

Sir Robert casually looked about the room before smiling at Igor. "I am sorry, Captain. I tend to speak a little too freely. Sometimes I should hold back and choose my words more carefully."

"No harm, Sir Robert," Igor replied.

Sir Robert continued. "We can do your country a service by taking at least one of the suitcase weapons off their hands. So you can see, this is the only possible scenario that could actually work. Everything else has been tried, from money to land to placate the parties involved with nothing truly succeeding. As for the Israeli's donating one of their weapons—they have agreed to do so but it is highly doubtful that the Arab Middle Eastern countries would accept a Jewish weapon preserving the peace. You understand the significance? That would not do in this case."

Igor nodded. "But what if we don't catch the terrorist in the US and he succeeds in his mission? What then?"

Sir Robert reached over to help Igor repack his bag. "Then, this meeting never happened —and I'm just an old man you had a leisurely chat with at the airport."

CHAPTER TWENTY

Annapolis, Maryland

Peter hoped to be in Washington by 2 PM, providing him with a safety cushion of a good five or six hours until his self appointed deadline of 7 or 8 PM. *No sense digging in broad daylight.*

One last prayer to Mecca—and only then would everything be set.

Ocean City, NJ

Turning to Boris, Forsythe placed his hand on his shoulder, wondering if they had come close to breaking it during the interrogation. "I would like to thank-you for the information, Boris, you have been a real help," Forsythe said sarcastically. "We are going to do you a big favor. The *we* being in the form of the United States government. *We* are going to allow you to walk. That's right, you can return to your little villa in Switzerland."

A look of shock spread across Boris's bruised face as he looked from agent-to-agent wondering if this were some type of trick. If it were, it would be consistent with the same tactics his FSB people utilized. Good cop for a few minutes or several hours then revert back to the original game plan and bad cop. Boris had told them everything he knew with the exception of where the remaining 30 suitcase weapons were buried. Then again why tell them? *They probably had no idea of their existence.*

"First things first," said Forsythe. "A trial would only bring out the sordid little details of your Russians suitcase bombs placed in the states. We don't want this juicy little tidbit of information reaching the press now do we? That would only incite a panic in the states, something we really don't need require at this juncture. So here's what I propose. We are going to escort you back to your fancy hotel where you will clean up and pack your bags. From there, we will escort you to Newark International Airport where you will board a Swiss Air flight departing at 7 PM tonight. Is this accommodating enough for you Boris?"

Boris managed a feeble smile for the first time his capture. "Michael, I do thank you for your understanding of this issue. This is something I will never forget."

"Boris, let's be honest shall we? You are pond scum. You are a low life that exists only at night when you crawl out from under your rock. I don't understand your rationale and hopefully never will. As a condition of your release, you won't be allowed to leave your villa except for food shopping and doctors visits. If you decide to leave for any other purpose, your old KGB and new FSB pals will be notified of your address. Last but not least, your phone will be monitored at all times so don't try and swing any more deals you may have rolling around in your head. That is unless you would like to talk to a few of our people? Do you understand what I have so generously laid out for you?"

Boris sat in the chair contemplating his conditions of release wondering what could be worse: prison or house arrest? "Michael you have my word that I accept your most gracious offer and stay within the confines of my home," rising from his chair, allowing the blood to circulate in his legs after having sat for the whole night handcuffed to the chair.

"As for you, Boris, I bid you farewell," Forsythe said. "I have a helicopter waiting to take me to Washington DC where we can put your little map to use," holding up the paper on which Boris had so diligently hand drawn a map which revealed the location of the suitcase weapon.

Boris allowed a brief smile to escape in response to Michael's goodbye, secretly knowing that the young rebel still had the capability to reach the second weapon in Philadelphia. The FBI foolishly suspended their questioning after finding out about the Washington weapon, thinking this would be the extent of the possible damage.

Another prominent case bungled by the FBI, thought Boris, looking Forsythe straight in the eyes, extracting some revenge.

So little did they know.

Annapolis, Maryland

The Americans will never know what hit them, thought Peter. It was time to thank Allah before entering the great Satan's capitol, for the devil was about to have its heart ripped from its chest. Peter wanted to pray for the third of the required five times per day for devout Muslims such as himself. He also required his strength, now more than ever.

The highway location would not be the wisest nor quietest spot for his prayers but this would be his last chance. He pulled off Highway 50 onto the emergency lane, slowing his truck to find a spot that would afford him some type of privacy, maybe by some trees or hedges. Only yards ahead, he noticed just what appeared to be an outcropping of hedges that approached the road, coming within 10 feet of the busy highway. He stopped by a road sign announcing that Route 495 lay two miles ahead.

Peter smiled. He was only hours away from eliminating the entire United States Congress, Senate, President and Vice President of the United States, along with 100,000 other souls already damned.

Sean Jackson sat watching the steady flow of traffic wondering how much his company would bank for the day. If his struggling company could keep its current pace for the next few months, they would pay off the very truck he was driving. *One down, two more to go.*

The business of car towing was cutthroat, with others attempting to hone in on your territory. Even with a signed contract awarded by the State, the Gypsy trucks were oblivious. The Gypsy trucks stole business wherever, whenever, they could. Due to this, Sean developed a good reputation with the State Troopers who patrolled the State Highway, calling in the illegal trucks as he spotted them. As far as he was concerned, they were robbing money from his family. Money he needed to survive.

Sean neared the end of a hectic 12-hour shift, patrolling Maryland State Highway 50 for his fledgling towing company—*Action Jackson Towing*. The *Action* in Action Jackson a toast to his nickname while playing football for the University of Maryland. A running back for the Terps top 10-ranked team until his leg decided to go one-way and his body the other. Until that last game, Pro scouts drooled over his quickness and pass receiving skills, a sure first round pick in everyone's playbook. No more. The injury ended his playing days.

With three late model trucks now on the road, Sean made the best of a Maryland State road contract awarded to him less than a year earlier. *Leading the nation in rushing for two years straight while at the University of Maryland still had some benefits*. Once awarded, he quickly secured a bank loan based on the expected workload and bought an additional two trucks to handle the new business. This shrewd maneuver enabled him to hire his two brothers and essentially keep it a family owned business.

Without fail, every time he worked the overnight shift his mind would drift back to his playing days. Dreaming of the *what if* scenarios. The multi-million dollar salary, the first class accommodations, the ability to hawk his autograph to the middle-aged yuppies on QVC.

Sometimes life doesn't work out the way you dreamed.

Since 1am, Sean had removed six disabled vehicles; assisted three motorists who had run out of gas, and even replaced an older woman's fan belt. With another day in the can, he looked forward to popping open a nice a cold beer back in the office.

Only three miles from the Route 495 intersection and his regular turn around point, he realized he had to check-in with his wife. God forbid if he missed a call. She would raise hell for days on end. It had to be like clockwork. At least five times a day, her wanting to know his whereabouts. His wife wanted him to know that safety lay only a phone call away. He never told her but he actually enjoyed checking in.

With 99% of vehicle breakdowns occurring in the emergency lane, Sean hung in the right-hand lane for his highway drives, making it easier for him to pull behind someone in need of his company's particular service.

Leaning over to pick up his CB, Sean checked the frequency for his office. "Action Jackson home base come in, this is AJ one talking to you." He hoped his wife was in a good mood after another long 12-hour day of working the office. He wanted to hire some additional office staff when they broke even later in the year.

Sissy Jackson met Sean in his senior year of college, and they were inseparable ever since. Sissy even nursed him back from his career ending injury, both mentally and physically. After graduation, with no real prospects on the horizon, it was her idea that they start a business of their own. Unfortunately, or fortunately, it depended on which one you talked to, the only business available for those with a limited amount of money happened to be a towing franchise. Sissy's father took a loan against his pension to provide Sean with the money to get started.

"Come in AJ one, I have a cold one waiting for you when you get back," Sissy cooed.

"Sissy, I should be back in the office in about 20 minutes. I'm nearing my usual turnaround point now," Sean said, before noticing a pick-up truck parked on the side of the road a couple of hundred feet ahead. "Scratch that Sissy, I have a broke," squinting as he pulled up behind the vehicle. "Looks to be a Black, Ford F-150. Let me give you the plate number in case he's a runner." It wouldn't be the first. Earlier in the morning, he filled a car with two gallons of gas only to have the driver take-off without paying. "It's a New Jersey Plate; five, nine, eight, zero, one." Sean paused, staring at the man on the side of the road. "Baby, you're not going to believe this, he's praying on the side of the road! Right here on Highway 50! This guy's got to be nuts!"

Sissy didn't like the sound of his potential customer, calling him right back. "Sean, just come back to the office, let one of the gypsy's handle him," her voice quivering. Something deep inside told her the situation was dangerous. "Do you hear me, Sean?"

Sean eyed the man for a few seconds more before responding back. "Sissy, he looks harmless enough. You know we need the money baby. Every job counts. I'll get back to you after I find out his problem." He put the mike down before keying it one more time. "And don't forget to keep my beer cold!"

"Sean, you take care! You hear me?"

Sean reached down for his trusty Swiss Army knife, placing it in his overall's pocket. It was the one tool he found to come in handy for everything but the large jobs, saving him countless time from routing around for the right tools in the back of his truck. He waited until the traffic lessened enough to enable him to open his driver side door, jumping out of his truck and hurrying across the front. He reached the grass as a big rig blew past.

Sean walked to within a few feet of where Peter kneeled in prayer, waiting to see if he would turn around in response.

"Hey buddy, you need some help or something," Sean said. "I'm the authorized service provider for this section of the road."

Kneeling beside the truck to hide from passing traffic, Sean had surprised Peter. He was getting ready to rise and continue with his journey before being rudely interrupted by this heathen. Nobody in his own country would have dared interrupt someone deep in prayer. They would have waited patiently until one completed their prayer before even uttering a word.

"What do you want?" Peter shouted, feeling his waistband for his 9mm before realizing he left his weapon in the truck.

Raised on the nasty streets of Baltimore, Sean realized the man was looking for his piece. Wanting no part of this crazy scene, Sean started to casually back up with his hands in the air. This was the one time Sean wished he carried his own piece. His wife told him on numerous occasions to carry a Colt

45 her father had given her, but he refused, thinking it would only lead to more serious trouble.

"I don't mean to interrupt you, my man," Sean said. "I just thought maybe your truck broke down. I'll let you get back to whatever you were doing." He kept walking backwards as he talked, a smile gracing his face as to not alarm the man. Upon reaching the passenger side of his truck he quickly flung the door open and jumped inside, sliding over to the driver's side. The flat bed revved up with no problem, producing a heavy, black cloud of diesel smoke as evidence.

Springing up from his kneeling position, Peter reached through the open passenger side window for his 9mm, seeing it was no longer there. He calmly but quickly opened the door, searching the trucks floor, finding it where it evidently fell when he had braked to avoid a careless driver a few miles back.

Peter now pointed the weapon at Sean as he sat in his truck.

Get a hold of yourself, Sean said aloud. "*You want to live another day.* He looked in his rear view mirror, then back to the man with the gun. Sean saw his chance with an opening in the traffic, applying his foot full force on the accelerator, his trucks rear wheels spinning in response, swaying towards the side of the road. When his trucks wheels finally caught the asphalt, he narrowly merged between a semi and a school bus.

Realizing he lost any chance for a clear shot, Peter ran along the grass strip still trying to aim his 9mm at the escaping flatbed. When the flatbed appeared once again in his gun's sight, a large semi-truck blasted its horn due to Sean merging his truck a little too close to his own.

This one action saved Sean's life as Peter glanced away momentarily, allowing Sean to move out of range of the 9mm.

Seeing he was free, Sean once again merged his truck to the outer lanes in order to escape the mad man. *What in the hell did I do?* Sean thought as he fumbled for his CB radio.

"Come in Action Jackson base," he screamed into the CB radio's mike, looking in his rear view mirror for the nutcase to suddenly pull up behind him somewhere. "Damn it Sissy, come in," Sean yelled again into the mike.

Sissy had just exited the bathroom when Sean's first request came across. She hurried back to the receiver in time for his second appeal. "Sean, this is Sissy. What's the problem baby?" She said slowly and deliberately.

"Some nut case just pulled a weapon on me! Can you believe that? He wanted to shoot me because I only wanted to help him! What's this world coming too?"

"It's okay, baby," Sissy said slowly, trying to calm him down. "Was this the same vehicle you provided me the plates only five minutes ago?"

That's right! He forgot about that. He could call the plate into the State Police and get this guy pulled over. "Sissy, I want you to call the State Police and tell them what happened. I want you to tell them it was a black, Ford F-150; you have the plates. It happened at mile marker 25 heading west on 50. The man was dark skinned, middle-eastern I think."

"Okay, I'm going to call it in right now." She realized he was too upset to grasp he could call it in himself over channel nine on his CB, the police emergency channel. "I want you to promise me that you will be back here as soon as possible. No more runs today; do you hear me? Turn that rig around and return to base!"

Sean couldn't agree more. This being the first time anybody had ever pulled a gun on him. "I couldn't agree with you more baby. I'm on my way home."

One mile back, Peter still stood by the side of the road, eying the passing vehicles before realizing he still held his weapon in clear sight for all to see. He quickly tucked the weapon back into his pants waistband before jumping back into his truck. As he did, Peter noticed the vehicle's CB radio mounted on the side of its dashboard. *This might come in handy.* He knew from his briefings in Syria that the American CB radios also operate a police frequency. *Another possible weapon to throw the police off his trail.*

Seeing an opening in the traffic, Peter carefully merged his truck back onto the highway, proceeding to Washington D.C. and immortality.

Officer Mark Lipatree of the Maryland State Police sat in an unmarked police cruiser west of the Routes 495 and 50 interchange, pulling speed checks. It was one of the two uneventful necessities of police work, the other being testimony in court. He couldn't complain, it was only his 2nd time in almost 30 days of "pulling speed" as his brethren would refer to it. Mark didn't mind the routine duty, even thought he preferred to be on patrol or street assignment. That's where the real action lay, catching the criminals and not your typical *Joes* who casually sped a few miles over the limit.

The mere presence of his vehicle provided enough of a deterrent for the speeders to slow down. *At least until they passed him.* No matter, this was *downtime* to him. It provided him with a few extra hours of time to study his computer programming course work. With only four years left until retirement, he hoped to have his degree in hand on the day he left the force.

Sitting in his unmarked car, he would occasionally look up to give the appearance of performing his duty. Sometimes even resetting the roof mounted radar unit to "shoot" a car or two. Only someone stupid enough to cruise by at ten miles or more per hour over the speed limit would find him giving chase. Most of the day would find him with a calculator in one hand and a well-used pencil in the other, trying to figure out his Advanced Calculus workload for his next class.

"Baker 12, Baker 12, we have a report of a man with a weapon," the women dispatcher stated in a monotone voice. "He is at Route 50, mile marker 25, now proceeding west. It's a black Ford F-150 pick-up, New Jersey Tags number five, nine, eight, zero, one. He should be considered armed and dangerous. Confirm please."

Mark placed his books on the passenger side of the cruiser, reaching for his radio mike mounted to a shoulder harness, having replaced the old, bulky dashboard mounted radios of past. "Rodger, Annapolis Center; Baker 12 will check out and report."

He expertly unsnapped the radar gun from the roof, tossing it casually beside him. As he shifted from park, a Ford truck matching the description sped by.

As he eased out into the highway, the traffic suddenly parted to accommodate his police vehicle. Driving an unmarked car, the driver of the pick-up would have a hard time identifying his vehicle, using all eight-cylinders of his specially outfitted Detroit cruiser to gain position. Mark fluidly weaved in and out of the traffic pattern, careful not to be observed.

"Annapolis Center this is Baker 12, I have the suspect Black F-150 under surveillance. The vehicles plate matches your numbers provided. I will attempt to pull over it over at Mile marker 30. Back-up would be nice with this one."

"Rodger that, Baker 12. Will have back-up made available," the distant, unseen female voice replied.

Slowing his police cruiser in order to position his vehicle behind the suspect's pick-up, Mark turned on the siren.

Having figured out the basics for operating the CB, Peter selected the random mode. This allowed the CB scanner to randomly search channels, picking up any transmissions that were made within its limited range. The first channel it stopped on picked up a conversation between two truckers whose accents placed them well below the Mason\Dixon line; they were discussing the high price of diesel fuel. On the second attempt, he found what he was searching for, a transmission between a base station and a police cruiser. Listening carefully to the discussion, Peter overheard them discussing a black, pick-up truck. He looked from side-to-side for any sign of a marked police car. Seeing none, he continued to listen to the conversation, losing the transmission briefly as he passed under the Route 495 overpass. As the transmission resumed, he saw a black car parked diagonally to the road off to his right, obviously a police car from its positioning.

In his rear view mirror, Peter saw the car quickly merge onto the highway and gradually ease its way up to just slightly behind his truck, off to the right. No doubt the police officer wanted to be absolutely positive it was the right vehicle. Listening further, Peter determined the police were going to attempt to pull him over at mile marker 30. Peter waited patiently until the next marker appeared. At that point, the car to his right moved into a position behind him, turning on his siren and lights.

Peter closed his eyes for a few seconds, appealing to Allah to intercede. *The unsuspecting police officer attempting to pull him over would be just another statistic in a few minutes.*

"Baker 12, this is Annapolis Center," Mark's radio barked as he maneuvered his car to within 20 feet of his suspect.

"This is Baker 12, come in Annapolis Center," Mark said in response.

"We have no back-up for you Baker 12—there is a major accident on Route 495 with two people killed. We have moved all available resources into the area for traffic duty. You are advised to proceed with caution. I can alert the DC police if chase proceeds into their jurisdiction. Sorry Baker 12."

Mark Lipatree could only shake his head. He was on his own. As he drove closer, Mark noticed a Police Association decal on the truck's cabin window. *This guys a cop?* He despised pulling over fellow officers—especially ones who had been drinking or involved in a domestic dispute. The badge would come out as if it were some magical ticket to freedom and then a weapon would most likely be shown next.

Looking in his rear view mirror, Peter could see the police officer moving into position. He needed a diversion. Peter accelerated to 85 miles per hour before swerving into the right lane, tapping a car's rear bumper, causing the car to swerve into another lane where it was promptly rammed by a truck.

Mark narrowly missed hitting the truck as he matched Peters every move, settling once more behind Peter's truck.

Peter knew the police in the United States had orders to break off high-speed pursuits, he decided to take advantage of the liberal law. Pushing the accelerator down to the floor, he quickly reached 100 miles per hour. He swerved into the lanes on either side of him before settling into the right-hand lane.

Mark was following Peter to the best of his ability, trying to avoid being the cause of another traffic accident. He decided to move across two lanes of heavy traffic and then into the emergency lane. This allowed him to avoid the burden of traffic and move up alongside Peter.

Mark toggled the cars mic. "Will the driver in the Ford truck, slow down and pull over," Mark ordered over his cars loudspeaker. "Don't make this any worse than it has to be."

Peter leaned over to his right-hand side to look down at the police cruiser before extending his middle finger. Using the truck as a weapon, Peter veered to his right, slamming into the police cruiser's driver's side door, causing the car to swerve up a grassy bank before correcting its path and veering back onto the emergency strip.

Once back on the road, Mark eased to the right and the rear of the truck, positioning himself for a tip maneuver he had learned in his Police offensive driving class only weeks before. Increasing his speed, Mark bumped his vehicle into the trucks rear quarter panel, causing it to swerve from right-to-left and then back again. As Peter tried to regain control, Mark pulled ahead and tossed a nail studded "road stopper" out his window and into the trucks path.

Peter saw the officer heave something out his window, unable to avoid it, he drove over it. He suddenly heard two loud, pops—his steering capability degraded dramatically with both tires on the right-hand side now flat. Peter steered over to the emergency lane—sparks flying from the now tireless rims. He had no choice but to stop. *Now he had to pick the spot to make a stand.*

The truck coasted to a stop underneath a roadway overpass. Peter looked in his rearview mirror to see the police cruiser pull in 20 feet behind him.

Peter removed the 9mm from his waistband.

Mark sat in his police cruiser mentally reviewing his own status—bulletproof vest, weapon loaded, pepper spray. Within a minute, his in-car computer produced a printout of the vehicle's owner. Looking over the information, Mark noted that this guy never had so much as a parking ticket. But there's always the possibility it was stolen and not reported yet. Just to be on the safe side, Mark unsnapped the top of his leather holster, freeing his weapon for easier access as he opened his door.

Approaching the 2nd minute since his forced stop, Peter was anxious. He realized that if the police officer received any kind of assistance, his mission would be over. Peter knew he could take care of one or two, but not the possibility of three or four police officers responding to his call. Sitting on the side of the road made him the proverbial sitting duck. Fingering his 9mm, he needed to make a move and fast. Opening his door with weapon in hand, Peter jumped to the asphalt roadway just as the police officer was exiting his cruiser.

Both seemed stunned for an instant, looking at each other as if in some macabre western gunfight. Peter had the advantage with his weapon already out.

Mark cursed loudly when he saw Peter with a gun in his hand. "I'm a Police Officer— drop the weapon—now!"

Peter fired first, hitting the driver's side door that Mark was using as cover.

Mark responded with three shots in quick succession. The first shot hit and shattered the driver's side window. The second and third bullets imbedded themselves in the doors steel cross ties.

Peter sought shelter in front of his truck, maneuvering around the still open driver side door and wildly firing two shots in the general direction of Mark to cover his run.

Mark cowered behind his cruisers door for cover as two more bullets flew harmlessly over his head.

Mark reached for his radio while scouting for Peter, seeing him ducking in front of his truck, using the engine block for cover no doubt. *He must have some type of military training because anyone else would have run by now, making himself a potential target. This guy is going to stay and fight.*

"This is Baker 12, repeat, this is Baker 12. Officer needs immediate assistance. Shots fired, repeat, shots fired. Highway 50, mile marker 30. Suspect is still armed."

"Baker 12 this is Annapolis base, I read you loud and clear. I have three vehicles on their way. ETA is 3 minutes. Repeat, ETA is 3 minutes."

Mark dashed out from behind his temporary cover of his vehicles door, moving to the rear of the suspect's truck. "Roger that Annapolis, three minutes," Mark replied. He lay down on the road to look under the truck. With the truck providing a 2-foot clearance from the ground to its frame, Mark viewed Peter's feet as he paced back and forth as if a caged animal searching for its master.

Mark took careful aim at Peter's exposed right foot, squeezing off two shots from his standard issue Beretta, hitting the wheel rim on the first shot and grazing Peter's foot with the second. Peter fell to his knees in pain, now on the ground in full view. Mark yelled for him to once again drop his weapon, taking careful aim, both hands on his weapon.

Peter could see the police officer pointing his weapon directly at him. Looking at his own wound he could see the bullet had just grazed him, nothing that should keep him from walking or running if need be. Peter assumed a runners start position with his weapon in his right hand flat on the ground. Looking back at the officer and then at this weapon. In one brief second, Peter made the rash decision to bring his weapon to bear and fire. Not taking time to aim, he emptied his clip by shooting under the truck towards where Mark lay on his stomach. Five of the six bullets hit the roads asphalt and ricocheted harmlessly up into the trucks rear cab. The sixth managed to hit Mark square in the chest, forcefully pushing his body up and slamming his head into the trucks rear bumper, knocking him unconscious.

Peter ejected the empty clip onto the highways hot asphalt, withdrawing a new clip from his waistband before professionally inserting it. Quickly looking under truck, his weapon ready for action, Peter noticed the officer lying sprawled on his back. Peter carefully made his way to where

Mark lay in the rear of the vehicle. Holding his 9mm in front of him, both hands locked together as instructed. He carefully peered around the trucks rear panel before seeing that the officer was indeed unconscious. Moving over to the fallen officer, kicking him once before prying the Officers 9mm from his hands.

Peter retrieved his bag, mockingly saluting the fallen officer. He tossed the bag into the back seat of the police cruiser as the traffic continued by, oblivious to what just transpired.

"Only in America," Peter said aloud as he pulled out into the heavy traffic that once again seemed to give way to the police vehicle.

Mark eased himself up from where he lay on the hot asphalt. A sudden pain in the center of his chest caused him to cry out in pain. Reaching down, he unbuttoned his shirt only to be rewarded with a deformed piece of lead imbedded in his vest, saving his life in the process. Eyeing the slug, Mark decided to put it in his pocket, a keep-sake for future reference. Looking about, he could see that both his weapon and police cruiser stolen. "Shit!" he said aloud. Reaching for his shoulder mounted radio, he called in his status, still looking around for his backup.

"Annapolis base this is Baker 12, come in Annapolis base," Mark said, his hand searching for the impact spot beneath his vest, one that would surely produce a grapefruit sized bruise in a day or two.

"Baker 12 this is Annapolis base. Your backup is in route. One minute ETA."

Mark wondered what in the hell he was going to tell his boss as he fingered his mike. "Annapolis base, Baker 12 has been shot. I repeat, shot. Vest stopped bullet." He fingered the bullet's bruise that made it difficult for him to breathe before continuing. "Annapolis base, my cruiser and weapon have been stolen by the suspect while I was unconscious. Please alert DC police that the suspect is probably heading their way." He stood up with the aid of the truck's bumper in time to see his back up maneuvering through the traffic, sirens blazing.

I am going to catch that bastard. And when I do—I'm going to kill him.

Three minutes passed since he left the officer along the side of the road. By now an all points bulletin would be posted. He knew the Americans did not take kindly to the murder of their police officers. Little did they realize, but this was already number two for the day—with many more to follow.

With the Washington DC city limits fast approaching, he wanted to ditch the police cruiser and steal another mode of transportation. No doubt driving a police cruiser would make it harder for him to blend in.

Driving past a Honda Civic, he noticed a young woman behind the wheel. Peter quickly hatched his next plan. Being in a police vehicle, he could pull over any car he chose; *couldn't he?* The Americans are a law and order society and would obey a police officer's command to stop. *That's it!* I could seize the vehicle of an unsuspecting person, someone naive or young enough not to ask questions. Someone similar to the young female he had just passed. *Brilliant!*

Wendy Wexler battled early afternoon traffic due to an accident slowing both sides of the highway. She was on her way home from attending morning classes at Montgomery County Community College. As she drove on Highway 50, she mentally reviewed her Physics Final she had taken that morning. She needed six credits to complete her Associates degree, and if she passed Physics, only one more course to go.

Turning to her right, she saw a police car slowing beside her. Looking down, satisfied she was within the speed limit, she went back to mentally reviewing her Final Exam.

Slowing to 50 miles per hour, Peter stayed in the outside lane, allowing Wendy's Honda to approach him. Peter slowed the car even further, gradually allowing her to pass. She glanced at him as she drove by. Peter pulled his car behind hers. He then noticed her nervously fidgeting in the driver's seat, looking from rearview mirror to the side mirror, and then slowing her speed to 50 miles per hour.

Peter had his victim—*now he just needed an appropriate area to pull her over.*

Looking ahead past the flowing traffic, Peter saw his opportunity in an off-ramp only about a ½ mile ahead. *It was once again coming together.* This would fit right into his plan. If he could get her to drive up the ramp and off the highway, they would be away from peering eyes.

As he drove, Peter searched for the switch to turn on the cars siren. In course he located the police radio. *Might be nice to have the latest on what type of reception they are planning,* he thought, fidgeting with the buttons on the radio. Giving up after a few seconds. Seeing nothing labeled for siren, he noticed a well-worn switch with no name affixed to it. Peter flipped the switch, and the siren sprung to life.

Wendy wondered why a police cruiser suddenly took up position behind her car. She wasn't speeding. The car was recently inspected, so her license tags weren't expired. She looked in the rear view mirror to notice the flashing lights first, followed by the siren. *My father's going to kill me if I get a ticket.*

Wendy looked immediately to her right in order to oblige the officer and pull over. Once again the traffic magically parted for both Wendy and Peter as he stayed behind her Honda, in effect riding its bumper with his vehicle as she made her way over to the emergency lane. Once in the emergency lane, she stopped 100 feet from the 14th Street exit ramp.

With two speeding tickets in the past year, Wendy knew the drill: show me your license, registration and proof of insurance. *Same routine.*

Peter couldn't help but notice the 14th Street exit ramp only a few feet ahead of the Honda. He had to coax his prey to drive the remaining distance up the ramp and off the highway to a more secluded location. He looked about the car's interior before finding a switch labeled megaphone. Peter pushed what looked to be the power button causing a green light to illuminate. Picking up the microphone, he pushed the detent a few times before hearing a clicking sound on a speaker outside of his cruiser.

"Will the young lady in the Honda please drive up the ramp and exit to the right? The traffic is too heavy for me to exit my vehicle."

Wendy heard the policeman's request to drive up the ramp, waving out the window in response. She then drove up the ramp at 10 miles per hour and exited as instructed.

In the meantime, Peter was able to figure out the police radio, turning it on in time to overhear radio traffic concerning the policeman he had shot few moments earlier. One particular comment piqued his interest. The officer he shot evidently survived due to his bulletproof vest, suffering only a concussion during the incident. An intense manhunt was now underway to locate Peter and the stolen police cruiser.

He didn't have much time. He had to ditch the cruiser and fast.

Peter followed Wendy into the parking lot of a single-story office building. He seized the opportunity and used the office building and the car to his advantage, pulling in beside her but allowing the office building to block his vehicles view from the street. He positioned the police vehicle out of view of anyone but Wendy. Peter then used the cruiser's megaphone to summon Wendy.

"Please approach with your registration papers and drivers license at the ready," Peter said. *He was ready to kill her if she didn't comply.*

Wendy gathered her documents and exited her car, walking in between the office building and the police car.

"Officer, I didn't mean to do whatever I supposedly did wrong. Please don't give me a ticket," Wendy pleaded. "I can't afford my car insurance as it is," she said, thrusting her documents through the open window at Peter. She looked down at his shorts and suddenly realized that something didn't make sense. She knew the police had undercover units, but they usually operated in the urban environments, not on traffic detail.

"Hey wait a minute, you don't look like a cop," slowly backing up as she said it. "Is this some type of joke?"

Peter pointed his 9mm at Wendy. "I don't think so."

Wendy started crying hysterically, holding onto the car for support.

"Stop where you are little lady," Peter ordered, exiting the police cruiser.

Peter took stock of the situation and looked in both directions, satisfied that no one could see them. "I'm not going to hurt you; you have my word. I only need you to provide me a ride downtown before I let you go. If you do as I say, this experience will be over in a matter of one or two hours."

Looking back at her car and then to Peter, Wendy's mind started racing. She had seen the nightly news and read the newspapers, young women such as herself were being raped and killed by people every day. She wasn't about to become another statistic. Fingering her car keys as Peter walked closer to her, mentally counting the closing distance—*6 feet, 5 feet, 4 feet......*

Peter kept his weapon at his side as to not frighten her.

She waited until Peter stood beside her before raising her can of pepper spray, directing the spray towards his face.

Peter was ready for her and instinctively blocked Wendy's hand as she reached out, able to dodge the worst of the spray, causing most of it to deflect back into Wendy's eyes.

She screamed in agony as the pepper worked its way into her tear ducts. She knew she had to get control of herself and the situation; she struck out once again by using anything at hand, striking Peter across his face with her ignition key. The cut started just above his right eyebrow and proceeded to his left cheek, the cut now bleeding profusely.

Peter grabbed Wendy, brutally slapping her across the face. Wendy slipped and fell into the rear quarter panel of her own car, opening a large gash on her forehead.

She screamed once more.

Peter had to control the situation and quickly. He patted her on the back, speaking softly to her as she lay on the ground.

Waiting several minutes for the effect of the pepper spray to wear off, Peter smiled at her as she looked up at him, admiring her lioness courage. *This one is a fighter,* he thought to himself. *She will do well in her future endeavors.* He could never hurt a woman brave enough to fight him in hand-to-hand combat, besting him more than any Russian commando had ever accomplished. She even drew blood, looking to his hand for evidence.

Peter smiled as he removed the car keys from her hand.

This time, Wendy put up no resistance.

His original thought was to kill her and dump her body. Her courage changed his plans. Gently lifting her up from the ground, cautious and ready for any action she may still take, Peter led her back over to the police cruiser. Once there, he pointed for her to sit in the driver's seat.

She hesitated at first before finally obliging, feeling a tight knot in her stomach as she did.

Peter produced a pair of handcuffs he removed from the cruiser, applying one open cuff to her left hand before threading it through the steering wheel and then cuffing the right.

"Sorry for the accommodations, but it is the best I can do," Peter said sympathetically, moving to the other side of the cruiser, smashing the police radio before removing the officer's shotgun and his own bag.

Looking back at Wendy as she struggled to try and remove the handcuffs, Peter admired her fight. He waved before driving out of the parking lot in her Honda.

Peter knew he would succeed—*for Allah had intervened once more.*

CHAPTER TWENTY-ONE

Dulles International Airport, Virginia

Walking comfortably among the crowd of business executives and vacationers, Captain Igor Isinov blended in as trained. Wearing Dockers and a plain white, short sleeve shirt, nothing bold or colorful that would cause him to stand out or call attention to himself. He looked the part of either an executive or tourist. Having arrived from London on the afternoon flight via Delta Airlines, he approached the United States Customs point. He knew from past experience that surveillance cameras were positioned at every conceivable angle to monitor the incoming passengers for possible terrorists or persons of interest. He placed a well-worn Baltimore Orioles Baseball cap atop his head and wore a pair of Ray-Ban nonprescription glasses to make it a little tougher.

The United States utilized the same identification software as their British counterparts, so Igor hoped for the best as he retrieved his forged United States passport from his garment bag. Admiring the navy blue document for a few seconds, one that identified him as one Jonathon Tresky of the United States, hoping the forgers of the Russian Special Service had once again performed up to their vaulted expertise.

As he approached Customs lines reserved for Citizens of United States, Igor tightly gripped his bag whose false bottom still contained his weapon and C-4 explosives. He chose to stand in line behind a boisterous tour group who seemed to have enjoyed the plane's beverage service just a little too much.

Igor could only appear dull after the Customs Agent processed this bunch.

The time spent in line was relatively short, with each person who stepped up to the customs booth given a cursory passport inspection; the agent passing the passports bar code through a scanner before each proceeded to the exit. The bar code would display to the Customs Agent a complete travel history of the person standing in front of them. Hopefully the real Jonathon Tresky was not wanted for any crimes in the United States, knowing that Russian operatives scoured American graveyards to establish a database of names and birth dates for use in their document forgers department. They sometimes overlooked the possibility that the person might have a criminal record. Igor heard of two FSB personnel serving time in the United States for crimes committed by the forged name for which they were using. Moscow reacted by setting up a storefront American credit agency, thereby enabling them to check certain backgrounds without suspicion.

When it came to Igor's turn, he walked up from his position behind the sign stating in big, bold letters, "Do not pass until called," smiling at the attractive, 40ish African American woman behind the plexi-glass partition.

"Passport, please," she said, having probably mumbled the same phrase for the hundredth time today. She looked at the passport picture then to Igor before running it through the bar code scanner.

"Mr. Tresky, did your enjoy your trip to," looking back at the passport, leafing through the well worn and stamped pages before locating the last stamp. "Russia?" She gauged him for any signs of nervousness.

"Yes, the weather is beautiful this time of year. No humidity like we have here in Washington," he replied truthfully—knowing Washington to usually feel like a swamp at this time of year.

"What was the purpose of your trip to Russia? Business or pleasure?"

"Pleasure, it was definitely pleasure. I have family in the area."

She cut him off with a wave of her hand. "Mr. Tresky, what hotel did you stay in on your last night in Moscow?

"The Hotel Metropolis," he shot back, knowing she would pursue further questioning about the hotel if he fumbled in any way. Igor was knowledgeable about the hotel, having stayed there on several occasions for mission related activities.

Satisfied with his response, the Customs Agent was about to hand over his passport when she looked back to her computer screen.

Igor started to worry. His bag began to feel as if it weighed a hundred pounds.

Focusing intently on her screen, she read something very carefully before picking up her phone to evidently quiz her supervisor, him in a booth 20 meters away. The supervisor looked in Igor's direction before speaking into his phone.

Igor's weapon lay at the bottom of the case, any sudden movement would be detected and he wouldn't stand a chance. He couldn't overhear what was being said until the Customs Agent thanked her supervisor and hung up the phone.

"Mr. Tresky, did you leave the terminal in London for any reason?"

What did the British do? Sir Robert said he would take care of his end.

"Yes, I went outside to have a smoke and grab a paper. You know the restrictions on smoking," he lied, hoping to strike a nerve.

"Don't I though. I could go for a smoke right now myself," she replied, waving him through the turnstile.

Nodding his thanks, he picked up his bag and proceeded down a 100-meter narrow tunnel that led to the outside of the airport and the airports cabstand. Igor said a quick prayer to St. John, betraying his Russian Orthodox upbringing, walking with confidence knowing the security cameras were still viewing him.

Halfway down the narrow hallway he heard a man's voice commanding him to stop—calling him by his alias— Jonathon Tresky.

Igor panicked for a split second. He could choose to ignore the command and make a run for it, seeing a row of yellow cabs parked no more than 20 meters in front of him. Before he could prepare himself, another Customs Agent suddenly appeared at the end of the tunnel blocking his escape to a cab talking into his radio as he viewed Igor walking towards him.

What went wrong? The passport was a beautiful forgery, a masterpiece; even Sir Robert admired the work as they sat sharing a beer in the London Airport.

The agent at the end of the tunnel was motioning for Igor to turn around and return to the customs control point.

Igor felt as if every camera in the tunnel were focusing in on him. General Poszk would not take his capture too kindly, possibly even disavowing any knowledge of Igor and his mission.

Igor prepared himself for the worst.

"Mr. Jonathon Tresky?" The first agent inquired, his hand positioned on his holstered weapon out of reflex.

Igor turned to face the agent, seeing yet another agent five meters behind him also standing with his hand on his holstered weapon.

"Yes, I am Jonathon Tresky. Why the sudden curiosity?" Igor replied, trying not to sound too sarcastic.

The young agent suddenly smiled, revealing a set of silver colored metal braces on his teeth. "You forgot your passport, sir," handing over the navy blue document to Igor's astonishment. "Sorry if we alarmed you, Mr. Tresky. You look as if you saw a ghost. Are you okay, sir?"

Quickly regaining his composure, Igor retrieved the passport from the agent's outstretched hand. "Thank-you," he said, holding the passport up and smiling. "I had something to eat on the plane that didn't agree with me." He patted his stomach for confirmation.

"Same thing happens to me when I eat burritos," the second agent replied. "I usually take a few anti-acids and the problem goes away."

"Thank-you again, gentlemen; I will take your advice," Igor said, quickly turning and walking down the tunnel to an awaiting cab. Looking up, he silently mouthed a "Thank-you," to the skies above as he burst out of the tunnel and into an awaiting cab.

"Russian Embassy," Igor said to the cab driver. "And take your time."

The Bell Jet Ranger Helicopter carrying FBI Agent Michael Forsythe landed at a make shift helipad set up at the National Mall, a mere 500 feet from the towering Washington Monument. Tourists lining up for the Washington Monument tour were caught gawking as the helicopter suddenly materialized in a hastily arranged landing zone, yellow police caution tape marking the extent of the blocked off area. The tourists wondered who the fortunate celebrity was to receive such a reception of two, Chevy Suburban's with a squad of black uniformed clad men in accompaniment, FBI emblazoned across their backs in gold lettering.

Forsythe used the helicopters 45-minute flight time to notify his home office of their desperate situation. He also set up a 3-block perimeter around the alleged bombsight, hopefully enabling them to seize the weapon before the rebel could remove it. Boris did inform them of the exact location where the weapon was located, but the suspect had a six-hour head start on them. The possibility even existed that he might have come and gone with the weapon. *Hopefully not,* thought Forsythe as he viewed the beauty of the White House only a mile away.

As quickly as the helicopter had disembarked its passengers, it was off and flying to the FBI Training facility at Quantico to retrieve additional bomb experts that might be required in the ensuing hours ahead.

One of the agents clad in black approached Forsythe and Thomson as they waved their thanks to the pilot.

Rocco Nelli's graying crew cut and barrel-chested physique greeted Forsythe along with a handshake and a pat on the back that would cause most people to lose their dentures.

"Michael, I have news for you," Rocco Nelli said before leading them to the Suburban where six men stood milling about. "I want to inform you that the President and Vice President have been evacuated to the Hills of Maryland and then head to Philadelphia in a few hours. The Congress and Senate were due back from summer recess today but we alerted them all to stay put until Tuesday." Rocco paused when he saw Forsythe wondering how he could keep the powers that be from their home turf.

"Gas leak," Rocco said in response, providing a toothy grin extending from ear-to-ear.

"Excellent job, Rocco," Forsythe replied.

Rocco Nelli was a gruff ex-marine drill instructor that joined the FBI during the military's *early out* program in the mid 90's, this due to cold war troop reductions. With only 13 years of active duty service with the Marines, he was eligible for a reduced pension if he left within two months. With his military pension safely in hand, he joined the staff of the FBI within 48 hours of his discharge, putting his experience learned in the Marine's Urban Tactics Team to good use, becoming head of the FBI's newly formed Urban Assault Team. Since that time, Rocco and Forsythe had teamed up on numerous FBI training scenarios and exercises, finding they meshed extremely well under pressure.

"I'm just glad you were available, Rocco," Forsythe said, looking at the team he had assembled on 30 minutes notice. Each looked as though they had just jumped off a Marine recruiting poster; crew cuts all, each in excess of 6 feet and 220 pounds. "I'd hate to meet your boys in a street fight,

Rocco." He then motioned his friend over to the nearest Suburban, spreading a map across the side of the vehicle.

"My boys are harmless, Michael. That is unless I don't feed them, then they become a little unruly. For our special mission today, in your honor—they haven't eaten yet."

A chorus of dog growls came from his men in response.

"Easy boys, it's almost time. I guarantee everyone a piece of raw meat when this is done," Rocco said, putting a half-smoked cigar in his mouth for full effect—looking as though he and his group were ready to storm an enemy held beach.

Pointing to the map, Forsythe stated the objective. "We have the gas company informing everyone for eight blocks around the Red Cross headquarters building that there is a gas leak. Of course, we all know there is no gas leak—*well at least now you do*. We need everyone evacuated while we hunt our target and search for a hidden weapon. Our suspect won't allow a gas leak to stop him. He has a strict timetable he must adhere to. So he will do anything to reach the rose garden beside the Red Cross building."

Anticipating a question from Rocco, Forsythe cuts him off with a wave of his hand. "I know what you are about to ask, so here goes my best attempt, short and sweet. In the late 1970's the former Soviet Union buried nukes the size of a suitcase on our soil to discourage any US first strike. The locations of the weapons were a secret until yesterday, when an old KGB agent disclosed the location of just such a weapon buried in the rose garden of the Red Cross building."

Looking from man-to-man, Forsythe could sense the professionalism amongst them. Not a man flinched—they just returned his steady gaze awaiting their orders.

Forsythe proceeded. "We presently have 255 agents positioned in an eight-block area around the Red Cross building and 250 uniforms for crowd control. That should keep the curiosity seekers out of the area. Now, our team will focus on the Red Cross rose garden. It's an area of only 50 feet by 100 feet, so nothing moves around it, or in it, that we won't be aware of. What I require from you gentlemen is a double shooting position on the roof across the street with another at street level in the mall area. Finally, I want three of you in the Red Cross rose memorial hidden amongst the various shrubs. Rocco and myself will check the garden for any recent digging and then assume a position in the building itself."

He looked from man-to-man. "I want to re-enforce the important issue we are dealing with here gentlemen. I have information he is heading this way, towards us. Only this morning in a remote Delaware State Park location our suspect killed an Atlantic City police officer in cold blood. To murder the officer he placed one bullet in his chest at close range while the officer was on the ground, probably pleading for his life. And less than two hours ago, our suspect shot a Maryland State Trooper on Highway 50, ten miles from our very location. Luckily our boy only received minor wounds and a damaged ego. But he is alive, and that's the important issue, *he is alive.* Our suspect is a shooter, gentlemen, he won't wait for you to set up and take your shot. Shoot first then ask questions people," holding up his hands to once again stem the expected questions.

"I know this differs from our standard policy, but this is a different situation. The rules have changed in our favor for a change."

The men let out a series of *ooh-rahs* in response, agreeing wholeheartedly with the change.

Forsythe continued. "Our latest intelligence has him driving a stolen police cruiser and heading to this very location. I think our boy is smart enough to have ditched the cruiser by now and commandeered another mode of transportation. What that is, we have no idea yet."

Rocco started to hand out flyers with the suspect's description.

Forsythe looked once again at his assembled agents, noting their youth and a vigor that he once possessed. He suddenly felt old.

To their left, the tourists were being ushered away from the Washington Monument by the DC police.

Satisfied that his warning was being heeded, Forsythe spread his arms wide like a preacher, signaling for the agents to gather around him.

"Now, no one knows about the weapons existence with the exception of you gentlemen and of course some of our superiors. Your fellow police and FBI brethren believe there is a dangerous gas leak, so let's keep the chatter to a minimum on the radio."

"If there are no questions, let's lock and load gentlemen, and may God be on our side."

A chorus of ooh-rah's could be heard by the still curious tourists as the men piled into their assigned vehicles, speeding off in a cloud of dust. The dust cloud drifted over to where the tourists were being escorted back to their vehicles, causing some to cover their mouths in response.

Little did the tourists realize—but the dust was the least of their worries.

Peter adjusted the cars' rear view mirror in order to look at the cut he had received courtesy of the *lioness*. He could see the blood had since clotted into a purple and red line. *Good*, he thought, deciding to keep the bandage off. *It will be easier to blend in where I'm going.*

Careful to maintain the speed limit, he had no desire to be pulled over for speeding at this juncture. After all, he was only eight kilometers from his intended target.

At this particular moment, he was probably more intimately familiar with the Washington road system then most DC taxi drivers. When his classes in Syria had ended for the day, Peter would study the areas of intended attack with the diligence of an engineer reviewing schematics. This enabled him to plan a variety of entrances and escapes, both to and from his target area, with him memorizing the various streets and highways around his target.

As he mentally checked off the exits leading to Pennsylvania Avenue, three Maryland State police cars sped past him in the far left hand lane, approaching what Peter could only guess to be in excess of 140 kilometers per hour. With their entering the Washington DC city limits, they were obviously in pursuit of him and the stolen police cruiser.

There was no way anyone could catch him now.

Wendy Wexler sat handcuffed to the steering wheel, wondering how the hell she had gotten herself into this unfortunate situation. Peter deliberately rolled up the windows, taking no chances of her screams being overheard. Not that it would be of any use with the area populated mostly by abandon buildings.

With the rising August temperature, Wendy desperately pulled at her metal restraints. If she could only break off a piece of the steering wheel, she could escape both the cruiser and the sweltering heat. After only five minutes, Wendy's wrists were raw and bleeding from her struggle.

Looking for any sign of life in the neighborhood, not able to notice so much as a cat on the prowl due to Peter's positioning of the car, Wendy shook her head in disbelief, cursing aloud. *What if nobody finds me?* Wendy had seen recent televised warning's not to leave children or pets in cars during the areas heat wave. With an outside temperature expected to reach the mid 90's, the local newscasters said that the temperature in some vehicles could reach 175 degrees in less than 30 minutes. At that temperature, a healthy individual would eventually succumb to a heat stroke in less than two hours.

Her mind raced with the thought of her poor father having to identify her body in the morgue. Wendy garnered all her strength in one tremendous effort, even propping her feet up against the dashboard for better leverage, before once again succumbing due to the pain in her bloodied wrists. Resting, she leaned against the wheel, causing the horn to sound loudly.

A smile creased her face at the sheer stupidity. *How did I overlook the horn?* Wendy slid the handcuffs up to the top of the steering wheel, enabling her elbows to depress the horn. She stopped every 15 seconds or so before starting again, establishing a pattern to *seriously annoy* someone in the area.

Two blocks from Wendy's location, Army 1st Lieutenant Sumeka Kellor jogged with Tongo, her 2-year-old German Sheppard in tow. Having already completed the park side of her daily 2 ½ mile run, she now weaving her way back through her neighborhood in order to complete her self-plotted circuit. Since returning from an Army posting in Germany, she couldn't help but notice how the criminal element had invaded what had once been a pleasant neighborhood, turning it into an area of rampant drug use and flagrant prostitution. With a well-endowed curvy figure and light cocoa skin, she was approached three times during her morning run by men mistaking her for a prostitute.

When she first purchased her three-story twin home, the area was close-knit, family oriented, with children able to safely play in the street and neighbors sitting on their steps in heated discussion about politics or the latest baseball scores.

Sumeka was lucky enough to have rented her home to a young, childless couple for the three years she served overseas. But they couldn't wait to leave, even informing Sumeka that they came close to breaking the lease due to the crime rate.

Times had certainly changed.

Now, Tongo was her protector while she waited until she could sell and move out to Virginia to be near the Pentagon—her new place of employment.

Sumeka was in no mood to deal with the criminal element that roamed her streets, still pissed over her car being broken into for the fourth time in the past month; the last time they even stole the new car alarm that she had paid $493 to install!

As she crossed Delany Street, Sumeka heard what sounded to be a car alarm or a horn beeping. Only this was different. Not sounding as if someone was stuck in traffic, this was more deliberate, almost a pattern. Standing on the street corner and looking at how far her neighborhood had fallen, she decided to make a stand, at least this once. Determined to catch the thief in the act, possibly the same one who had vandalized her own car, she ran with Tongo in tow towards where the sound emanated. *It's not going to happen again, not in my neighborhood*, she said aloud, a mad scowl upon her face.

Three teenage boys, each no more than 15 or 16, stood in her way on the concrete sidewalk, plying their drug trade.

They had no problem noticing the attractive Sumeka, the oldest boy flashed a smile as she made her way into the street in order to avoid them.

"Yo baby, slow down, come on over here and pay us a visit," said the oldest boy, blowing her a kiss, followed by an obscene gyrating gesture with his hips."

Sumeka ignored him as she walked past.

"One day your gonna be without that damn dog, then what you gonna do?" said another before turning back to ply his lucrative crack trade, hi-fiving his fellow teenage dealers.

The sound was getting closer, even with the traffic noise of Highway 50 hanging in the air. Sumeka walked to where the street met with the Highway 50 on/off ramp. Puzzled, she stood looking both ways before she determined that the noise was coming from behind the only business left in the area. Her Army training took hold; Sumeka knelt down beside her dog Tongo, petting her softly.

"Girl, I want you to go check this out before me?" She searched her dark brown eyes for some type of understanding, unhooking the dog's chain. "Go girl, go," pointing the way for Tongo, watching as Tongo first jogged then broke into a sprint, Sumeka close behind. As they turned the corner of the building, it became apparent that it was a police car, but not a DC police car— its dark blue strips identifying it as a State Trooper. *Why would they be here? We have city police protection.* Calling her dog to heel beside her, Sumeka could see a young woman in the driver's seat. Sumeka knocked on the driver's side window to get the girls attention.

Wendy turned to face Sumeka, a sense of relief flowing over her thinking she was about to be rescued.

"Are you okay?" Sumeka said, motioning with her hands for Wendy to roll down the window.

Wendy responded by holding up her handcuffed hands. She nodded that she was okay before slumping on the steering wheel in apparent relief.

Sumeka stepped back, wondering what the State Police had one to her. The girls face beaten and bloodied, her clothing disheveled. She could see the girl's hair matted on her head, wet from perspiration. This was no way to treat a prisoner.

"What did you do to get arrested? Sumeka said, already feeling sorry for the woman.

"No, no," Wendy said, shaking her head, panicking that Sumeka might leave, thinking she was under arrest. "Some madman kidnapped me by posing as a police officer. Please, get me out of her," she said in between sobs. "I don't want to die in here."

Tying Tongos' leash to the car doors handle, she looked about the immediate area for something, anything to break the window, settling on a 3-foot piece of cast iron pipe that lay against the doctor's office wall. With the Doctors office being at the edge of a highway and in a seedy neighborhood, it was only natural for it to become an illegal dumping ground for trash.

Sumeka held up her hands to try and calm her. "Honey, everything is going to be okay. I want you to turn away from me and face the passenger's side window," pointing over to the other side of the car. "I'm going to use this pipe to break the window," holding it up so she could see it. "Some of the glass might hit you but don't worry, it's a special glass and should only spider," using her hands to draw a web on the window. "Its safety glass."

Wendy nodded before turning away.

Sumeka stepped back to get some leverage before executing a swing the Nationals would be proud of, smashing the DuPont safety glass on the driver's side into a spider web pattern.

She then used the end of the pipe to push the lightweight window harmlessly into the police car, in the process just missing Wendy as it slid in between the driver's seat and the door.

"You all right, girl?" Sumeka said, reaching in to touch the bruises on her face. "You said something about being kidnapped?"

Wendy let out a sigh of relief at being rescued. "Yes, a man pulled me over using this police car. He identified himself as a cop and then beat me up and stole my car."

"First things first baby, we can call 911 and get some real cops down here," Sumeka said, patting Wendy on the shoulder for reassurance.

"They will nail that bastard for sure."

CHAPTER TWENTY-TWO

Highway 50, Outside Washington DC

Officer Mark Lipatree could still feel the sting of the slug that nearly penetrated his bulletproof vest. Of course, paramedics showed up as a standard procedure for a police shooting, bulletproof vest or not. Also on site, his supervisor and battalion chief had each scrambled to the scene when word reached them of an "officer down".

Mark sat in his chief's cruiser. Shirt still unbuttoned, empty gun holster beside him on the passenger side—he waited patiently for his chief to provide him with the latest information from headquarters.

Chief Sanders walked over to Mark, leaning in the passenger side window. "The FBI is sending a helicopter to pick you up so you can help identify the man who tried to plug you. They say he's the prime suspect in a couple of high profile crimes including the killing of one of our brethren just this morning. From what they told me, you're lucky to be alive. This boy's considered a cold-blooded killer."

Mark broke out into a cold sweat, his heart racing upon realizing how fortunate he was to still be alive.

The Chief's radio sprung to life. "Chief Sanders, come in please, this is Sky Bug One looking for a spot to place my baby," said Jimmy Hawkins, his blue and white Bell Jet Ranger hovering 2 miles out over Highway 50. As an ex-Army Special Forces pilot, Jimmy had years of experience landing in many a tight spot.

The Chief searched the sky for the helicopter, before sighting him directly ahead. "Rodger that Sky Bug One, we have a field to the north of the highway that is ready for a landing, no wires or obstructions are evident," said the Chief, motioning for Mark to move over to the field for pick-up.

"Rodger that Chief, I have you in sight and am now moving into position for my passenger pick-up." In less than 15 seconds his helicopter plunged from 1,000 feet to ground level, his passenger, Richard Knox, choked back his breakfast in reaction.

"Did you like that landing, Rich?" Jimmy said. "What do you say we do it again? I think I screwed up when the tail swung around too far."

"No, freaking way you clown," Richard Knox shot back. "You're a damn nutcase, you know that?" He jumped out of the helicopter, walking over to where Mark stood waiting in a field of tall weeds.

"Hi, I'm FBI Agent Richard Knox," Richard shouted above the rotor noise, extending his hand, "You must be Officer Mark Lipatree."

"Yes, sir," Mark said, shaking Richard's hand, following him into the still running helicopter.

"This here is the one and only Jimmy Sanders, our illustrious pilot for the ride," Richard said, motioning to Jimmy, him waving in recognition before pushing the stick forward and rapidly rising off the ground.

Richard could see the look of fear on Marks face, realizing it was his first ride in a helicopter as his hands searched for the seat belt.

He smiled in response to Marks actions, realizing he wasn't the only one who disliked helicopters.

Richard pointed to the pilots left indicating his next stop. "Mark, we have one more passenger pickup and then we land on the Washington Mall over by the Washington Monument."

Mark provided him a thumbs up before turning to vomit on the floor.

"What are you doing?" Forsythe said abruptly to the young rookie cop after he allowed a man on a bike to head back into town. "Are you handicapped? Did you understand your orders? Nobody is to enter this area, only exit. Do you hear me?"

The young officer cadet had been pulled from the Washington DC Police Academy training class to complement the officers already on duty, assisting in the massive effort to evacuate the three-square block area of downtown.

"Yes sir," he replied sheepishly, looking away from Forsythe before turning back once more. "But sir, the man had to go get his dog. He didn't want to chance being away for several days due to the gas leak."

Shaking his head, Forsythe put his hand on the cadet's shoulder, physically turning him to view the departing traffic. "Do you see which way the traffic is going, cadet?"

"Yes, sir," he replied, wondering if this was going to affect his class grade in anyway, possibly hindering his graduation the following month.

"It's heading out of town, not towards town," Forsythe said, restraining his temper. "From this point on, nobody goes into town without an FBI agent's specific order. Is that understood?"

"Perfectly, sir," he replied, eyeing first the traffic then Forsythe.

Turning back down Pennsylvania Avenue, Forsythe knew his men were already in position around the Red Cross building. Additional FBI agents would surround and provide back up in the immediate area with DC Police on call at the outer ring.

The terrorist would have to be a magician to enter or escape unscathed.

They already knew the rose garden lay untouched.

Forsythe realized the suspect now had to approach them.

The trap lay set—time to await the mouse.

The embassy reception room where Igor sat waiting patiently for the FSB Station chief to show was an overwhelming site when first viewed. Dark Mahogany wall panels provided an elegant backdrop to the floor composed of imported Thai teak, resembling a wealthy persons reading room or library from the late 1800's, only the stuffiness and odor of decaying paper were absent. With no windows to allow natural light into the room, brass floor lamps were positioned strategically about the room to enable one to fully enjoy the room's interior.

"Old Bolshevik" memorabilia lay scattered about. Blood red flags adorned with gold embroidered hammer and cycles spaced every five meters or so, each intertwined with Russian flags, each two meters by one meter in size. The symbolism of both flags intertwined was not lost on Igor. He next observed several metal hammer and cycle sculptures on a shelf to his left and then just past them a total of ten, three meter by three meter red star banners previously used in the Moscow May Day celebrations. Igor felt stuck in a time capsule from the 70's or 80's, when the old USSR was at the pinnacle of its power curve.

As Igor rose to view a glass case of Faberge eggs, Colonel Sergey Vasov, FSB Station chief, made his grand entrance into the room. Colonel Sergey Vasov would be hard to miss in a crowd, with him standing at 6 foot 6, 250 pounds, looking as though he could fill-in as a linebacker for the Redskins football team. Sergey and Igor were old friends, both having graduated from the same class at the Frunze Military Academy. Igor was also Sergey's best man at his wedding.

"Igor, how are you my friend," Sergey said, embracing him in a bear-like hug.

Igor stood staring at his friend for several seconds admiring his friends rank badge, finally reaching over to comically brush it off.

"I see you've been promoted once again," Igor said, impressed with his friend's movement through the ranks, something he could never achieve due to his mischievous conduct, having already been reduced in rank several times. "Congratulations, I cannot think of a person who deserves it more," smiling at his friend. "It has been too long since we fought the Afghan's, I think it was 87."

"It was May, 1988," Sergey replied with a serious tone about him. "I remember the month and year specifically, with my war wound forcing me to seek treatment back in Moscow."

Both laughed aloud at the mention of Sergey's "war wound," the wound received in an impromptu soccer game when he tripped on one of the many rocks that littered their playing field.

Igor pointed to the wound badge on Sergey's tunic. "Is that what you received this for?" He shook his head in mock disgust.

After the laughter subsided, Sergey motioned for Igor to take a seat once more, looking to get down to the business at hand. Only two hours had passed since Sergey had been informed of Igor's impending visit by General Poszk. He was also ordered to provide Igor with any assistance he required.

Any assistance.

Sergey reached into his black leather briefcase, extracting a business-sized, tan folder from its interior, placing it on Igor's lap.

Igor glanced at Sergey and then back to the envelope. "I suppose you would like me to open this?" holding the folder up for him to see.

"It's Christmas, Igor. Make a list, check it twice; that sort of thing," Sergey replied with the standard joke at the embassy.

Inside the folder lay a single sheet of paper listing various munitions and weapons stored on-site at the Embassy, and available for his personnel use. Igor opened the folder to look at its neatly typed contents, seeing everything from AK-47's to anti-aircraft missile's.

"As you can see, we keep available quite an arsenal for any potential problems we may encounter. It all comes into the country via the diplomatic pouch, or in this case the diplomatic crate," smiling as he said it. We both play the game, the United States ships in the same products we do. You are familiar with the game better than anyone, Igor. The cold war never truly ended. It is similar to a miserable marriage or divorce, the mistrust still evident in their dealings with each other.

Igor nodded as he scanned the list. Settling on three fragmentation grenades, a foldable stock Uzi, and a Motorola handheld radio/scanner, before handing the list back to Sergey.

"I need that within the next 15 minutes, is that doable?" He knew his friend to be extremely resourceful when it came to the art of scrounging. Igor remembered one particular holiday they had spent in Afghanistan. Being in the field, the traditional food served by the military cooks was something of the canned surprise variety and usually cold by the time it reached you. After a month of this same, boring routine, Sergey traded a broken, unusable jeep to a local chief for three goats and 10 pounds of cheese. They lived like kings for the next week, the envy of everyone else in the unit. Yes, if anyone could acquire what he needed, it would be Sergey.

"I can have it waiting in the lobby by the time you get downstairs. Quick enough?

"You haven't changed a bit."

I will take that as a compliment, Igor," both rising from their chairs. "We will both meet when your mission is over and have that drink you owe me," he said as his military aide entered into the room, walking directly over to where they both stood.

The enlisted man stopped five meters short of the Colonel, holding up a red folder with "Top Secret" emblazoned across its top.

"Colonel Sergey Vasov," the enlisted man said, snapping to attention. "You have received an urgent message from Moscow. It's to be read immediately."

"Bring that folder over here, Sergeant," the Colonel ordered, looking at Igor as if to apologize for his man's actions. "This man beside me is an Army Captain who probably possess' a higher security clearance then myself."

The enlisted man walked over to Igor and executed a perfect 45-degree angle salute as if on a parade ground. "My apologies sir, I was not informed of your presence in our embassy."

"None required, Sergeant. You were only performing your duty," Igor said, impressed with the soldiers sincerity, returning his salute with a more casual one.

He turned to hand the Colonel his folder, the Sergeant once again executing a perfect salute before turning to withdraw back to his post in the message center.

"He's a good man, Igor. He keeps his mouth shut and does what he is told," Sergey said, anticipating a smart remark from Igor. "Allow me to open this first and then we can continue," holding up the folder.

After several minutes, he looked up at Igor, handing the message for him to read. "It is from General Poszk, he informs me that you are aware of one of our many little secrets. On this side of the ocean, I tend to call them our *Devils Suitcase* instead of suitcase weapons. Suitcase makes it sound as though we are traveling to some overnight destination. *Devils Suitcase* are a more accurate portrayal of their intended use."

As FSB Station Chief, Sergey knew the location of each *Devils Suitcase* dispersed throughout the United States. Up until he received the message from General Poszk, Igor's true intentions were not revealed to him, only that he support him any way he could. Now, the general chose to include Sergey in the inner circle with the disclosure of the problem with the Washington DC weapon. Something was amiss.

Igor read the message in the folder and in-turn informed that the American FBI knew of the problem with the DC weapon. It was to be considered compromised according to communications intercepted by the FSB.

The FBI were using the weapon as bait and attempting to trap their rebel.

Peter pondered the repercussions that could be expected for something of this magnitude. Maybe it could actually work to their advantage? This would be a small price to pay considering the end result. It would also put an end to the plan Sir Robert and the General envisioned, but at least the rebels would not control it. That would seem to be the most important aspect of the situation, at least to Igor.

"I see our FSB boys are still the best at intercepting communications," Igor said, re-reading the message.

Sergey looked uneasy. "I find myself in the position of having to apologize to you my friend," he said. "It seems as though we might have a problem. A little over an hour ago, the DC police closed an 8-square block area of the city; something to do with a gas leak. I was monitoring the situation due to one of our weapons being smack dab in the middle of the leak area. With the general's timely message and yourself being here, it looks as if something else is brewing.

"Hold on, Sergey," Igor said, realizing that with the gas leak story and the area cordoned off, the rebel might smell a trap and pass. He now wondered if the rebel had an alternate weapons location. *The damned FBI, why couldn't they just let him walk in unobstructed and then nab him? It could be over in a matter of minutes instead of drawing additional attention to the area.*

"Sergey, the FBI is basing all of this on our rebel only having one location, one suitcase. This man is going to have a backup plan—he'd be a fool not to."

Igor assumed he did and would have to leap ahead ASAP to try and spring his own ambush at the next location. He would allow the FBI to guard and then retrieve the DC weapon. The new scenario would work to Igor's advantage, sweeter than the original planning.

"I need you to tell me the location of the two closest weapons in proximity to Washington DC. If I am correct, I feel our rebel might choose to abandon this area and move to a less intrusive location, one absent both the FBI and police. If I can anticipate his next move and beat him to the next location, I could possibly ambush him. The game would effectively be over."

Sensing the urgency in his friend's voice, Sergey was already heading for the rooms exit. "Follow me."

The Capitols majestic white marble dome came into view as Peter turned off the Highway onto 13th street, only two Kilometers from his first objective. Eyeing the dome caused a shudder to run through his body with the realization sinking in.

From Peter's previous discussions with Boris, he had stated the suitcase weapons initial blast would destroy the surrounding area up to and including the Capitol itself. The resulting explosion would effectively saturate the Capitol in a radiation bath, and provide a slow death for the unfortunate souls inside.

The light turned to red, allowing Peter to view the faces of people who potentially could be affected by his actions. He fixed his gaze on a group of young children crossing in front of him, evidently on some type of a field trip. They held onto a single rope to not get lost, the last child in line stopping to wave at him as he sat in his car. The little blond haired girl giggled as she strove to catch up with her group, her adult teacher now hurrying her across the street before the light changed.

It's more than that, thought Peter, trying to block the mental image of the children. This one blast would cripple the United States, wiping out its White House, Treasury, Supreme Court and many other minor, but never the less prominent cogs to support its government's existence. It was a mission to save his own countries children and their families. It was war, and in a war people had to die.

Peter focused on the plan. Once the suitcase was removed from its earthen tomb, he would adjust the unit's timer for 10am the following Monday morning—this would allow maximum exposure of the weapon—catching most at their work areas. *The big fish would also be in the pond.* From news clippings and published schedules that were available on the Internet, the President would be giving a speech on the White House lawn at the same moment. This would allow the world to view the resulting explosion live on the Television a mere fraction of a second before the cameras melted from the searing heat that would accompany the thermal blast.

As he drove down 13th street, Peter noticed the heavy volume of traffic coming from the opposite direction—away from his target. Sensing something might be amiss, he searched the car's radio for a news station. After several tries, he found one that kept running the top headline story of a gas leak forcing an eight block area around the White House to be evacuated.

"Damn it," he said aloud, banging his hand on the dashboard. Peter realized the Red Cross building was only two blocks from the White House.

He decided it would be more advantageous to ditch his car and scout the area around his target— maybe the gas leak could work to his advantage. Remembering what the Russian said in his emails, he described the area he would be digging in as surrounded by 6-foot tall arborvitaes. The arborvitaes would in essence provide him camouflage at street level. Since it was Sunday, no one would be in the offices to see him. *Perfectly planned.*

Finding a parking spot for his borrowed auto was easy enough, pulling into a liquor store parking lot on the gas closure perimeter, then choosing to abandon the vehicle.

His objective lay only eight blocks away.

CHAPTER TWENTY-THREE

Washington DC

With the pilot's skilled touch, the helicopter dropped capably from its 2,500-foot altitude to land mere feet from the rear gates of the White House, directly across the lush lawn from the Red Cross Headquarters building. At any other point in time, the Mall would be a virtual beehive of activity with football and soccer games and everyday people picnicking on its grassy expanse. With the gas leak's evacuation, it emptiness resembled a 1950's "B" movie scene after the effects of a nuclear attack, the exception being the numerous police officers strolling its concrete sidewalks.

Wendy Wexler sat beside Officer Mark Lipatree in the back seat of the helicopter, having enjoyed her first ride, laughing at the sudden drop in altitude.

Mark sat beside her— sick and pale from his own helicopter experience.

Jimmy Sanders turned to Mark and Wendy, applying his best southern accent and said: "Ya'll come back now."

With their arrival, the noose had slowly tightened around Peter's neck.

The office looked typical for an American business executive, with an oak desk topped by a laptop computer, plants hanging around the perimeter and a backdrop of family pictures neatly arranged behind the desk. The photos were the usual: kids posing in their baseball or soccer uniforms, the family at Disney World, his deceased Mother and Father. The only problem was it belonged to Colonel Sergey Vasov, of the Russian Embassy.

"Sergey, I worry about you," Igor said as he looked about the room. "I think you are becoming too immersed in the American culture," pointing to the family picture at Disney World.

"Kids, Igor, kids. They love it over here," Sergey said as he removed a key from a chain around his neck, inserting it into a file cabinet lock, allowing the top drawer to open. He searched his color-coded files before carefully extracting two from the drawer, one green and the other purple, laying them on his desk for Igor to see.

"Langley, Virginia and Philadelphia, Pennsylvania," he said matter of factly. "They are the closest locations to our DC weapon."

"It has to be Philadelphia," Igor said confidently. "Langley is too close for comfort, the whole DC area is crawling with FBI and police with this gas leak story. It would also put our man on a direct path to New York and an international flight home. That has got to be it."

"I'm heading to Philadelphia. I will require some background information on this," pausing as he looked down at the folder for the exact location, "Fort Mifflin," a puzzled expression breaking out on his face. "Is this really an American Fort?"

Sergey allowed a slight laugh to escape. "At one time yes it was, but that was over 200 years ago during their American Revolution," Sergey replied. "Now, it is a tourist destination. Being the American history buff that I am, I have visited the Fort several times."

Satisfied with Sergey's response, Igor felt the target would be lightly guarded, if at all. "Very well, have my items available and downstairs in five minutes," Igor said, before realizing he was outranked. "I'm sorry Sergey; *please* have them downstairs in five minutes."

"Remember your pay grade," Sergey said jokingly, brushing aside his friend's comments. "And I will throw in a set of night vision goggles due to darkness settling in by the time you reach your destination, that and a detailed ordinance map of the area should do nicely."

"You're like a mother hen," Igor said, putting the file in his garment bag.

"I do have some additional information they may not have informed you of in Moscow," said Sergey.

Igor nodded. "Hit me with it, my friend."

"Setting up one of these devices is complicated. The bombs require a small amount of power to keep them safely in storage. We had to run a very small wire to an electrical source, such as an overhead power wire, and then attach it to the weapon. The wires are small enough that they would easily break if someone tampered with them or tried to follow them to their source. But in case there is a loss of power, there is also a battery backup."

Sergey produced a small Lithium Ion battery from his pocket, the battery no bigger than two decks of cards stacked one upon the other. "If the power wire was damaged in any way, you would have to replace the existing battery with one like this."

Sergey handed Igor the battery for examination.

"Do you think our rebel is aware of this?" inquired Igor, carefully pocketing the battery when Sergey instinctively turned to look at his ringing phone. Igor would require the battery if he were to safely remove the weapon for the Generals and Sir Robert John's peace plan.

Sergey ignored the call, tuning back to face him, him shrugging his shoulders. "Just catch this thief," his mouth spitting out the words as if he had tasted something that did not agree with him, "and when you do, kill him." Sergey could only think of his own family, safe in Woodbridge, Virginia.

Igor smiled at Sergey, seeing his friend had not lost his passion for a fight after his many years in the United States.

"That's my intention. *Either him or me.*"

Michael Forsythe had conducted his final security check of the surrounding area. He now walked with a bruised and battered Boris in tow, having gone back on his word on letting him go free. After Forsythe had flown out of Ocean City with Jim Thomson, a second helicopter returned for Boris and the remainder of Forsythe's team. Forsythe knew Boris required some form of hope to hang onto, thinking his freedom could be bought. Boris was still valuable—he had intimate knowledge of what the suspect looked like. Forsythe could keep him out of view until needed. Boris was also within the weapons range if detonated. Forsythe thought this might encourage Boris to possibly be more forthcoming with any additional information he may have held back.

The slightest possibility existed did exist, so Forsythe was taking no chances.

As the FBI helicopter approached, Forsythe realized his reinforcements were in-hand. Two additional bodies that could help identify the suspect, and not a moment too soon.

"Boris, wait here," Forsythe said, calling over a DC policewoman.

"Miss, I want you to watch this man and make sure he doesn't move," Forsythe said, pointing towards the battered Boris.

"Be a good boy Boris and maybe I will let you go home after all," turning to walk the 100 yards to where the helicopter was in its final approach.

Boris smiled at the policewoman, nodding his head in a polite greeting before tuning to watch Forsythe walk towards the helicopter.

He fixed an all-knowing gaze on Forsythe before laughing aloud. *You have no idea where he is going after this, do you my friend? I will be long gone before you realize you have lost a major city.*

The policewoman thought the old man had a screw loose.

Boris turns back to her, still smiling. "I must apologize for my outburst, I just thought of a joke that a friend of mine told me yesterday. I would tell you but you would probably find no humor in it." He turns back to watch Michael greet his guests. "It's concerns an old Russian joke from long ago that is now coming home to roost, right here in the United States," still maintaining a smile. "I'm sure you will be hearing about it soon."

"Welcome ladies and gentlemen," Forsythe said to Wendy and Mark above the din provided by the rotors, nodding to Jimmy and Richard in the same instance.

"Jimmy, keep the motor going, I want to take a quick look over the scene," shouted Forsythe, pointing to the air above them.

Jimmy responded with nod.

Helping Wendy step out first before noticing the mess on the floor at Marks feet, Forsythe could see the Officer was white as a ghost. "You okay, Officer?"

"I am now," he replied stepping out and onto the level grass lawn, his knees buckling slightly.

Forsythe held his tongue, remembering his own first experience in a helicopter 15 years before. The pilot was a cocky Vietnam vet who decided to pull a few fast maneuvers to spook Forsythe. It turned out to be the wrong thing to do because Forsythe relieved himself of his morning's meal, leaving a nice mess for the pilot to clean up. Unfortunately for the pilot, somebody learned a fine lesson that day, *and it wasn't Forsythe*.

"I want you two to follow me over to the briefing area where I can go over a few ground rules before I deploy you to the surrounding area. You two are our spotters."

They walked over towards where Boris stood beside the policewoman.

Forsythe could see the Russian still providing him that same silly-assed smile despite all that had come to light.

He knows something, thought Forsythe, picking up the pace—*that bastard knows something*!

The perimeter around the *gas leak* was loosely guarded, having had only an hour to implement. But it was the best that could be arranged on such short notice. With each passing moment, it would only get tighter as additional workers were brought in to assist.

Aware that the security perimeter had to be breached before the area was indeed "locked down," Peter lacked the luxury of time. Choosing to walk along the edge of the security zone, he scouted for a potential entryway, probing for a weakness. Having infiltrated many a Russian combat line, he was confident he could penetrate an incompetent American security barrier.

Peter walked along the perimeter, easy enough to identify due to the strategically placed police cars positioned every 1/2 block or so, he immediately spotted a weakness. He had to exploit it before the police became suspicious of him walking just outside the zone. It was only a matter of time before someone would question his intentions.

As he approached his targeted entry point, Peter overheard two police officers in their parked vehicle arguing about the upcoming Redskins football season.

In the heat of their argument, they hadn't noticed him.

Peter realized this was his opportunity, ducking behind a large elm tree for cover.

From his position, he could see the police car 20 meters away parked half on, half off the sidewalk. Just five meters beyond their car lay what looked to be a service alley. That would be his objective, the alley. It must lead to some sort of business or an apartment building. A second elm tree just behind their car could only help provide cover as he moved move into position.

It looked as though they weren't paying much attention to anything but themselves.

Peter checked his weapon then stepped out from behind a large elm tree, keeping parallel to the next elm tree and using its angle to eliminate the officer's rear view mirror as he approached. Reaching the next tree placed him only five meters from the police car.

"But I'm telling you the Eagles don't have an offensive line. How can they even challenge the Redskins for the Division title?" asked the first officer.

"You don't know what the hell you're talking about," the second officer replied, obviously disagreeing with this point.

This was his chance. Peter fell to his hands and knees and crawled over to the rear of the car. Once at the back of the car, Peter took a deep breath to calm his nerves, thinking that it couldn't be this easy. Hearing the discussion heat up again, Peter saw his opportunity, crawling the remaining five meters to the service alley. Once at the alley's entrance, he ducked out of view of the street. He decided to keep his weapon at the ready, unaware of who he might encounter. Scanning the immediate area, he was able to see down the garbage strewn service alley to what looked like the kitchen delivery entrance for the Washington Hotel, only 2-1/2 blocks away. Picking up his pace, he jogged the remaining distance to the propped open rear door, choosing to enter the hotel via its empty kitchen area. *No doubt evacuated for the gas leak.*

Peter was now within the perimeter and moving forward. From his studies of the immediate area, he knew the

Washington Hotel afforded him the best vantage point of the Red Cross building, located directly across from the Washington Mall. He would only have a wide expanse of green lawn between himself and his objective.

Running past the neatly hanging stainless steel pots and pans in the quiet kitchen, his weapon at the ready, he searched for the stairs or a door to the lobby area. Seeing the door leading to the restaurant, he burst through, scanning the room before maneuvering around the deserted tables. As he walked past, he could see remnants of the afternoon brunch still laid about, its diners having abruptly departed with the gas scare.

Exiting the restaurant's main door brought Peter into the atrium lobby, a waterfall providing the only noise in what was one of Washington's most popular hotels. Peter decided to slow his pace.

It turned out to be a wise decision.

Less than 20 meters from his position, Officer Lester Maddox stood by the hotels glass front doors, he was peering through his Minolta binoculars at a helicopter attempting to land on the Washington Mall. With the sudden evacuation of the hotel's occupants and staff, Officer Maddox provided security for the hotels safe. As he stood watching the helicopter his radio suddenly sprang to life.

The radio transmission also startled Peter as he cast a wary eye about the lobby looking for additional security. Following the radios sound he was able to locate the officer. Peter looked about for any additional officers before over hearing the officer say he was "still alone."

That was a fatal mistake, thought Peter. *He just handed me the key to the front door.*

As the police officer signed off the radio, he resumed viewing the helicopter with his binoculars, something to pique his interest on what was sure to be a long, boring day.

With the Officers interest fixated on the helicopter, Peter eased through the lobby, his gun focused on Officer Maddox as he crept closer, the lobbies' waterfall providing a soothing background noise to mask any sound of his own.

Walking past the front desk, Peter kept his weapon trained on the Officers back as he glanced about the room, not wanting to be ensnared from behind. Satisfied the area was indeed empty, he moved to within three meters of the Officers position.

"Put your hands in the air and no one will get hurt," Peter demanded, the waterfall providing the only other sound in the Italian marbled lobby.

Officer Maddox responded immediately, placing his hands in the air, holding the binoculars aloft in his right hand. "Don't shoot man. Take what you want and beat feet out of here," he said. The Officer responded as trained, immediately giving in to the man's demands, buying time until he could find his own weakness on the man.

Peter nodded. "Walk backward away from the door and don't turn around." He wanted to keep the officer off balance and out of sight from any help that may arrive via the street.

"You know the area's surrounded," Officer Maddox said before complying with Peter's demands. "There's a major gas leak in the area, this hotel could blow up at any moment." He was trying to use some basic psychological tactics on Peter, thinking he was a common criminal trying to take advantage of the situation and steal the hotels money.

"Yes, and I am Peter Pan," Peter replied sarcastically. "Don't make any sudden moves or I will use this," reaching in to remove the Officers weapon from his holster, surprised it was an older style 45 caliber. Peter saw another opportunity arise. The officer looked to be about the same weight and height as himself.

Again, Allah presents himself.

"Take your clothes off and hurry. I don't have time to rationalize,'' Peter demanded, watching as the officer quickly complied.

Peter removed the binoculars from the Officers hands before using them to view the helicopter.

Looking back, the Officer had his clothes in hand.

"Drop them at your feet and take ten paces backward and no one will get hurt."

"Come on, buddy," he said. He hid a canister of pepper spray in his hand under the clothes. "I'm standing here in my damn underwear. What the hell could I do to you?" He tried to entice Peter to come within range of the spray, the effective range being only eight feet with Peter now about 15 feet from the Officer.

"Just take the clothes, would you? He held them at arm's length as he started to walk closer to Peter's position at the door.

"Stay where you are. One more step and you'll be a dead man," Peter said, aiming his weapon at the officer.

The Officer could see the man was serious, dropping the clothes to the floor with the pepper spray at the bottom of the pile—the canister providing a dull metallic thud as it hit the marble floor.

Walking over to pile of clothing, Peter reached down to remove the Officers handcuffs from his uniform belt. "Turn around and walk towards the front desk."

Officer Maddox followed his demands, proceeding to the front desk. Peter took the handcuffs and attached them to a brass foot bar at the base of the check-in desk and then to the Officers left wrist.

"This should hold you until I can get away," Peter said. He walked over to the pile of clothes and started to undress and exchange them for his own. After several minutes, Peter placed the officer's hat upon his head completing the transformation, resembling a newly minted Washington DC Police Officer, the only exception being the pants being too big around the waist.

"You should go on a diet," he said, holding the pants out before tightening the belt to pull them in.

"Yah, I'll take that under consideration," said Officer Maddox. He looked embarrassed as he stood in his boxer shorts against the front desk.

Walking over to the front door, Peter focused the binoculars on the helicopter then back to the group of people meeting before the Red Cross building. Applying additional magnification, he refocused in on the people in the group.

"You bastard!" Peter said loudly. He viewed Boris, Wendy and Mark in the group talking to an FBI agent. "I thought Boris was a true patriot," focusing in on his face and seeing the bruises that were now visible and then noticing the handcuffs. He quickly changed his mind. "No, they made him talk. Sorry my Russian friend, but it looks like you will be serving a long prison sentence."

This situation was now compromised. That was easy enough to rationalize. Peter had to reach Philadelphia before the next weapon was moved into *protective custody*. If under duress, Boris might reveal the plan for his own entry into Philadelphia to lessen his sentence. Peter needed to think fast. It was a matter of pure survival—his own. Focusing the binoculars back to the helicopter, Peter could see that it was still running and evidently waiting for someone. Shifting his gaze 100 meters ahead of the helicopter, he saw a police officer walking a post pattern as if on guard duty. Peter looked down at his uniform then back out the door to the waiting helicopter.

"I would like you to meet, Boris," Forsythe said to Wendy and Mark. "He is one of the gentlemen responsible for all of today's actions. You have him to thank for your unfortunate predicaments."

Wendy and Mark both eyed Boris as if he were the devil himself. Wendy walked up and kicked him in the shins before Forsythe and Mark could restrain her.

"Please, miss," Forsythe said as he held Wendy from behind, her legs still lashing out in defiance to Boris. "The three of you will be working together."

"I'm not working with him," Wendy replied, her eyes burning with rage.

"What I require from you right now is teamwork until we catch this guy," Forsythe said, turning her around to face him. "Now calm down little lady, we don't have much time," waiting until she closed her eyes and started to tear up, the rage still building.

The woman police officer that held Boris by the arm noticed a fellow officer walking across the Mall towards where the helicopter was running. Thinking something was amiss she reached for her radio to place a call to her supervisor.

"Charlie this is Carol, can you tell me if we have someone patrolling the east side of the mall across from the White House?"

Overhearing her radio call, Forsythe turned around to see what she was referring to, seeing a police officer only feet from the helicopter, holding his hat against the rotors forceful winds. "What's the hell's going on there? He said aloud.

Wendy and Mark turned to see the police officer by the helicopter reach up for the door, letting go of his hat in order to do so, providing them a full view of the police officer's true identity when his hat blew off.

"Oh my, God," Wendy said, letting out a scream. "That's him! That's the man who stole my car and beat me up!" She now pointed to the man entering the helicopter.

Mark had the same thought as he joined Forsythe in running towards the helicopter, weapons at the ready.

"We have the SOB."

Peter felt exposed, almost naked, as he walked across the street and up onto the Washington Mall, continuing towards the helicopter. Looking straight ahead and keeping his focus on the helicopter Peter could fell the adrenaline flowing through his veins, providing him with a powerful rush.

Not taking any chances, Peter sprinted the remaining distance reaching the helicopter's rear door as the whole crowd turned to look at him.

Forcing himself into the helicopter, Peter quickly placed his gun to Jimmy's head before he could respond with his own weapon. "Get this bird into the air in two seconds flat or you are a dead man," Peter said, pressing the cold steel in to the base of his skull.

"You got it, boss," Jimmy responded, trying to stall a bit, seeing Forsythe running to his aid. "I just need to trim the blades for a few…."

Peter cut him off by firing a bullet through the co-pilots portion of the windshield before pointing the weapon back at Jimmy. "I said now!"

The helicopter lifted off just over the heads of Mark and Forsythe as they pointed their weapons skyward wanting to shoot but knowing that an agent was on board.

"Damn it," Forsythe said, running back to where Boris was standing, still smiling. "You know something, now spill it."

Boris nodded, feeling the situation having changed dramatically in his favor, holding up his hands to be uncuffed.

"Michael, can we now make that deal?"

"Uncuff him," Forsythe ordered, knowing he would eventually regret his decision.

"You will fly at 1,000 feet," Peter said, his free hand frisking the FBI pilot before relieving the pilot of his standard issue 9mm, placing it on the seat beside him in the back. "You will maintain a northeast direction until you see Highway 95, you will then follow that route north," Peter ordered. "No sudden deviations."

"Come on boy, what do you think you're going to accomplish?" Jimmy said, wondering what the hell was going on. "Why don't we set this bird down and have ourselves a little talk and see if we can resolve whatever issue is bothering you."

Peter responded by reaching over Jimmy and turning off his helicopters transponder, which would have allowed air traffic controllers to follow the helicopters path and thereby direct assistance to Jimmy. He then pulled the radio mike off Jimmy's head, cutting any chance of Jimmy secretly allowing the air traffic controllers to monitor what was being said, possibly providing them clues of what direction he was flying.

"I don't want you to say another word for the duration of this flight," Peter replied angrily, firing another shot through the co-pilots window for emphasis, the guns noise in the close confines of the cockpit deafening. The bullets trajectory closely followed the first, allowing the cool air to now flow freely through the two small bullet holes in the windshield.

Nodding his head in understanding Jimmy saw the Routes 95 and 295 interchange below, wisely steering the craft as directed, following 95 north.

Peter also saw the interchange and grinned, knowing that he could still complete a portion of his mission.

His message would still be the same but with less potency.

This was his last and final chance.

CHAPTER TWENTY-FOUR

Highway 95 - Baltimore, Maryland

The traffic flowed steadily for a summer Sunday evening, placing Igor only 90 minutes from his next destination in Philadelphia. Before he left the embassy, Igor asked his friend Sergey to keep a close and personnel eye on the fluid situation involving the *Devils Suitcase* at its downtown location. If Sergey saw the weapon was removed by the American FBI and not the terrorist, the better for Russia and the world.

Igor realized Sergey had his connections and could possibly swing a visit to the area. At least if the FBI had possession of the weapon, Russia could protest via diplomatic channels for its eventual return. It would be considered a major political embarrassment for Russia but hopefully it would be kept "close hold" between the countries spy agencies.

Careful to maintain the speed limit, Igor didn't require any unnecessary attention at this juncture of the mission. The Russian Embassy vehicle he drove came absent its customary diplomatic plates, a generic Maryland plate added in its place. The 2014 Toyota Corolla also had its trunk loaded with grenades, an AK-47 with cursory ammunition, and night vision goggles. That along with his personal 9mm would be a police officer's dream stop. Right up there with a major drug bust. The newspapers would have a field day with his background and his Russian Embassy ties.

Approaching the first of two rest areas, Igor saw a highway sign announcing city mileages: New York - 142 miles, Philadelphia - 53 miles. Igor reached over for the file on Fort Mifflin that Sergey had provided him. It was time to get acquainted with the area surrounding his destination. Pulling into the busy Maryland House Restaurant parking lot, he would pause for a few minutes and scout the best approach to take.

He had less than an hour to reach his target.

Peter constantly monitored Jimmy's actions as he maintained his 1,000-foot altitude; below them lay Baltimore Harbor with its ships at anchor or heading out into the Chesapeake Bay. It had been an uneventful 10 minutes since Peter fired the second bullet through the Helicopters windshield to gain the pilots silence. He heard tales of hijacked airliners whose pilots conversed with their hijackers, leaving the radio on to relay to ground controllers their precise location.

That wasn't about to happen.

The Air Traffic Controllers no doubt tracked him on radar. The ground controllers were informed of the hijacked helicopter by his FBI supervisors and clearing a traffic path for him, *at least he had hoped so*. With his transponder being in the off position, the helicopter would be hard to locate.

What really worried Jimmy was his present course; he would approach Philadelphia's International airport and hence another heavily congested airspace. He had to say something even if he was ordered to keep his mouth shut.

Half-turning in his seat, Jimmy could see Peter pointing his weapon at him, indicating for him to turn around.

"Look, buddy," Jimmy said. "I have to tell you about the area we are heading into," pausing to see if Peter would stop him, hearing nothing in return he continued. "When highway 95 approaches' the city of Philadelphia, it runs parallel to the cities International Airport. That's a lot of heavy-duty air traffic. It would be wise to avoid that area. I can plot us a new course…..,"

Peter cut him off.

"Enough," he said, knowing exactly where they were and what they would encounter along the way. "Do you actually think I would allow you to provide us a course? What kind of fool do you think I am? Keep your mouth shut and fly. You have performed well up to this point; I would hate to see anything happen to you."

Jimmy realized time was running short and he had to take some type of action. He would have to attack when they landed or even while they were in the process of landing.

Yes, that's it, while they were landing.

Forsythe stood toe-to-toe with Boris in front of the Red Cross building. He wanted information, and he required it immediately.

Boris smelled a deal. It had to be a foolproof deal; one that would grant him immunity and transportation back to Europe, having already missed his reserved flight the night before.

Forsythe brutally pulled Boris aside, away from the gathering of people on the sidewalk. He did not require their conversation to be overheard. Satisfied that they were safely out of earshot, Forsythe dug his claws in.

"Boris do you remember our little conversation?" Forsythe said referring back to the torture he had to endure.

He remembered it very well, allowing his hand to traverse the cuts above and below his right eye. He still experienced difficulty breathing from the blows to his stomach, possibly breaking several of his ribs in the process.

"Yes, Michael, I will remember it for the rest of my life," Boris said. He now stared directly at Forsythe, knowing he truly held the upper hand this time, unlike earlier when Forsythe performed the old bait and switch. Promising him a quick return home in trade for his information on the Washington DC weapons location.

"But now, I want a commercial flight out of Dulles." Boris looked at his watch, realizing that a Swiss Air flight was departing in 3 hours. "And I want to leave now. I will provide you the location of where our friend is flying to when I am safely aboard and granted Diplomatic Immunity."

Forsythe grabbed Boris's jacket lapels, pulling him in close. "Look here you sad excuse for a human being. I'm trying to save thousands if not millions of lives from being lost," throwing him to the ground before kicking him once more in the ribs.

Forsythe looked back at the group of officers and agents who were watching the impromptu interrogation; he could see the look of disapproval only from the uniformed officer. His agents were ready to restrain the uniformed officers if need be, knowing the importance of the information Boris possibly held.

Forsythe reached down to help Boris, pulling him up, brushing the grass clippings off his clothing. "Boris, I will put you on the plane personally if need be. You can be home at 27 Alter Strasse, in Bern, Switzerland by tomorrow morning."

A look of surprise spread across Boris's face concerning his personnel address, one that he thought a closely held secret. "How did you locate my home, Michael?" Boris said, his voice cracking.

"We have our friends around the world, Boris," Forsythe said, now taking his own turn at grinning."

Boris rubbed his hands over his ribcage in obvious pain, his earlier bravado having vanished.

"I want your personnel guarantee of my safety, Michael," Boris replied meekly.

Forsythe put his arm around Boris to help him walk due to his busted ribs. "You have it, scouts honor," Forsythe said. "But I will require the information right now, none of this waiting three hours bullshit."

Stopping a few feet short of the group, Boris turns to Forsythe, the pain showing upon his face. "If you are aware of my new address, that means the FSB is also aware." His expression now turned to one of fear.

"I would say that this is a high probability, Boris," looking to his assembled group who stood awaiting their new assignments before turning back to Boris. "Do you have a new request you would like to make at this time?

The sun beat down upon Boris's exposed head as he stood facing Forsythe, the sweat once again beading on his brow, the cut above his eye feeling the sting of its salt content. He hoped to avoid Washington DC and its unbearable humidity on this trip, but other forces of nature had taken that possibility out of his hands.

"I want to enter your witness protection program," he said, wiping the sweat from his brow, careful to avoid his open wounds.

The request seemed reasonable from his end, but Forsythe allowed Boris to sweat some more, wondering if he had anything else of value to provide before answering. The longer he waited, the more Boris would sense rejection and drop some more bait for him to bite. Standing in front of Boris, staring down at his pathetic figure hunched over to one side in pain, Forsythe realized there was more. His honed instincts of being in the FBI for 25 years told him there was additional information to be garnered.

"Speak and I'll listen. You have two minutes to tell me what is going on here and then where the rest are."

This was an unseen blow, one that caused him more pain than the shot to his ribs. Boris was getting too old for this type of work, knowing his life expectancy was now considerably shorter if he returned to Switzerland.

"They are heading to Philadelphia, or just on its perimeter," Boris said. "The Muslim gentleman is going to detonate one of our devices at a historical Fort up there. Fort Mifflin."

Forsythe nodded. "Okay that piece of information has bought you access to your bank account in Switzerland." He knew more was forthcoming. "Keep talking."

Boris managed a smile. "He will detonate it at 8:35 PM," he said, his breathing shallow from the broken ribs. "If you call your Secret Service you will have confirmation that your President will have just landed in Air Force One at the adjacent International Airport. It was planned that way in case he was missed in Washington."

Forsythe spoke rapidly into his cell phone, able to confirm that the President would indeed be flying into Philadelphia at the time mentioned. His next call was to his superiors, telling them to get on the horn and move the president. He also needed another helicopter.

Turning back to face Boris, he said. "We'll talk about the other weapons when I get back." He then motioned Jim Thomson over.

"Our new found friend here is about to enter the witness protection program. See that he is taken care of."

"Until we meet again, Boris," said Forsyth.

"Until we meet again, Michael," the pain in his ribs causing him to take shallow breaths, "and thank-you."

"Okay," Peter said, pushing the weapon into the base of Jimmy's scull. "I want you to land in a park coming up on your right hand side," forcibly pushing Jimmy's head to one side in order to look in the direction he was pointing.

"All-right, I see it, you don't have to be nasty about it," Jimmy replied. He could see a business parking lot and a patch of green alongside the Delaware River, still some four miles short of the airport itself.

"Land this piece of junk now!" Peter said with his weapon still in place, ready to use it if the need arose.

Jimmy slowed his helicopters forward speed to achieve a landing on a small patch of land, one that was surrounded by trees and power wires that could only make his landing even more hazardous.

No problem, thought Jimmy as he purposely overshot the first landing attempt, causing Peter to pistol-whip him about the head in response.

"I'll give you one more chance," Peter said, once again placing the gun at the base of his skull.

Jimmy was stalling for time. During the ride up, he had informed Peter the maximum speed he could achieve in the aging helicopter was 85 knots or the engines would blow. Of course, this was a lie; the helicopter could achieve 130 knots on any given day. It was just one of Jimmy's tactics; fortunately for him it worked. Saving the best for last he still had the landing to look forward too. Realizing that only the pilot and co-pilot seats were built to be shock absorbent to accommodate a hard landing, he could steer the craft into a semi-controlled crash. This presented the possibility of disabling Peter as soon as they were on the deck. That was his last and only hope.

Peter realized Jimmy was trying to stall for time. "If you don't land this helicopter in less than 30 seconds, your brain is going to be splattered across the windshield."

Jimmy half turned in his seat, facing down the gun barrel that was now was in his face, smiling at Peter in the back seat. "No problem, my friend," forcing the helicopter into a steep dive before leveling off swiftly at 250 feet to make sure he could maneuver clear of the parks many tree's.

"Now," Peter demanded, firing once more through the co-pilots windshield.

"You asked for it," Jimmy said, bringing the helicopter down at a rate of descent four times higher than recommended by the manufacturer. At this rate of speed, the helicopter was hard to control even for a veteran pilot such as Jimmy, as the helicopters tail rotor swung around and hit an overhead power line—slicing the line in two and cutting the power for the 500 or so people in the immediate area. With his tail rotor disabled, the helicopter swung wildly in a tight circle before crashing into a 75-foot oak tree. Luckily for its occupants they survived the initial crash with the tree's canopy assisting the helicopter by stopping the top main rotor from its dangerous spin, causing it to come to an abrupt stop and imbed itself in a 10 inch overhead branch. From there the helicopter essentially slid down branch-by-branch the remaining 30 feet to the ground. The impact of the ground on the cockpits aluminum structure was immediate, pushing the structure inward and crushing both the front pilot and copilot seats, decapitating Jimmy instantly.

With Peter positioned behind Jimmy, he was able to use Jimmy's body as a shield and rode the remaining distance down essentially on his back of his seat.

It didn't take long for a small crowd to gather around the mangled wreckage, curiosity keeping them at bay due to the downed power lines wiping around like a 4th of July fireworks display. It would only a matter of a few minutes before Police and Fire services would arrive on the scene.

Peter awoke to find himself lying on top of the pilot. He could feel something heavy lying across his back but he was unharmed. Reaching behind him, he was able to forcefully grab and push a jagged piece of the aluminum craft off his back and extract himself.

Peter had only one objective at this point, to reach his rental car he had pre-positioned only 200 meters away. His detailed planning had him position a second rental vehicle on one of the many side streets in the small town of Essington, which happened to be six kilometers south of the airport. He recognized he eventually would have to pass through on his return from Washington and would want to switch to a "clean" untraceable vehicle for his next phase of the operation. Little did he presume that his mode of transportation would be a helicopter.

Staggering out from the distorted aluminum mess, Peter took a few weary steps, trying to regain his balance, blood flowing from a head wound. Taking one look back at the wreckage before starting to walk away—*Peter realized he was lucky to have survived at all.*

Several of the crowd that had gathered were now attempting to extract Jimmy from the wreckage, not knowing the FBI agent already lay dead. The rest of the crowd pointed towards Peter as he now jogged away towards his pre-positioned car.

He had to hurry; he could hear sirens wailing in the distance evidently heading to the crash scene.

The area of Essington where Peter had placed his rental car contained a mixture of small businesses and town homes. This combination allowed Peter's car to go unnoticed and not arouse the suspicions of its neighbors. Jogging across the street from the park, Peter was able to seek shelter in a vacant storefront as the first police cars arrived on the scene. Watching from his vantage point as the ambulance arrived right behind the police. It was only a matter of minutes before the bystanders would inform the police of his escape from the wreckage.

The sight of his rental car brought a sigh of relief to Peter, removing the advertisement for a local deli that someone had placed on his windshield before getting in and quickly driving off. Careful to obey the traffic laws, Peter stopped his new vehicle for a stop sign, this allowed the passage of several additional fire fighting vehicles. Peter managed a smile, knowing he was only minutes from the Fort and his end goal.

CHAPTER TWENTY-FIVE

Fort Mifflin, Philadelphia, PA

Another beautiful summer day with the temperature in the low 90's albeit with high humidity. But it was summer—he could be shoveling snow or battling ice. He didn't want to rush the seasons. *It was the end to a perfect day*, thought Tom Giacono, a private security guard working at Fort Mifflin as he waved goodbye to the Forts daytime volunteer staff. Having experienced one of the largest crowds ever for a Sunday, Tom was looking forward to a little "down time" and relaxing down by the Forts south wall, one that ran parallel to the Delaware River.

Tom had placed a cheap wooden rocking chair he had bought at Kmart on top of the forts earthen wall in order to view the ships passing by in front of him, mostly oil tankers and small pleasure craft. He would break the rocker out after the last of the staff had left in order to not disturb the historical surroundings while the tourists still muddled about.

His shift started at noon and would end at midnight, when he would be relieved by Charlie the midnight-to-noon guard. Until then, Tom would pass the remaining six hours by waving to the people passing by in their pleasure boats. Of course since he was the security guard, he would also perform his customary walk around the Forts interior every hour on the hour and check the doors and windows for any sign of break-in. Not that anyone would want to break-in to an old Fort.

Having recently retired from his city job where he had worked for 45 years, Tom approached his 66th birthday in stride, feeling and looking as if he was a robust 56. Sporting a pronounced beer belly on a short frame, salt and pepper graying hair with an accompanying waxed mustache; *he looked like a typical grandfather.* With his wife, Denise, they planned an around-the-world cruise for the following year. This was the main reason for him taking the weekend security position at the Fort; to earn the drinking and side-trip money with his part time gig. With his children spread around the country and no grandchildren to speak of as of just yet, they thought this would be the ideal time to slip away for four months and really enjoy themselves.

From his perch, Tom looked over to his right and observed the aircraft taking off and landing at the Philadelphia International Airport.

Life is good, he thought, leaning back in his chair. *Life is real good.*

The Philadelphia International Airport lay off to his right hand side as Peter's car exited Highway 95. Soon the president's jet would join the aerial circus in jostling for prime position. Of course his jet would take precedence over the commercial variety, with the airport virtually shutting down 10 minutes before and after his specially configured 747 appeared in the landing pattern.

It was easy to navigate the back roads that wound around the airport and towards his objective, Fort Mifflin, following the historical markers conveniently placed about.

Driving past the airports east side, Peter noticed elaborate steps already being undertaken to guard the various approaches to the airport. Secret Service types now patrolled the airports fenced perimeter, easy enough to identify by their cheap suits. The local National Guard units were also assisting with vehicles parked every 25 meters or so along the fence line to handle the crowds that would suddenly materialize before the Presidents aircraft arrived.

Peter drove past the last of the "weekend warriors," still following the historical markers leading to the Fort.

After 500 meters, he drove through a stately bank of maple trees that occupied both side of the road driving slowly towards the Forts impressive brick and earthen structure. It would be a shame to destroy such an honorable piece of history, thought Peter, parking his car next to the only one left in the gravel lot, most likely the security guards. But such is war. People are killed and places destroyed. Brutal, but human nature.

With the hour approaching 6:30 in the evening, the sun was still high in the western sky, thus providing Peter with plenty of light for the work he had yet to accomplish. It was perfect timing as he glanced down at his watch. If he could set the weapon for 8:30, he would have the President of the United States in his crosshairs. The president along with the targets the old Soviet Union programmed to be destroyed back in the 70's; the vast complex of oil refinery's on both sides of the river, the International airport and the old US Navy base, now since deactivated but two mothballed carriers in its lonely port just the same. With close to 500,000 people living in the bombs immediate range, a major catastrophe was in the making. Not as impressive as the Washington DC weapon's kill zone, eliminating practically the whole government, but this would be just as deadly.

Peter removed a trenching shovel he had bought at an Army/Navy surplus store from his trunk. Boris had informed him that the weapon lay buried only one meter below ground. With this information in hand, he could have the weapon out of its dirt grave in the matter of an hour or so.

Peter gained his bearings from the evening sky before heading towards the Fort.

It was time to get to work.

It was Igor's turn to traverse the same ground that Peter had undertaken only an hour before, now approaching the Airports east side. As he did, Igor began to encounter heavy traffic, both pedestrian and auto. He also noticed a heavy police presence, this along with military troops stationed along the airports perimeter fence line. His mind raced. What if his rebel had already set the bomb in motion?

Spotting an older couple that was pausing to allow his car to pass, Igor pulled up alongside them, rolling down his window. "Good day, sir," Igor said in his best-polished English. "Could you tell me what this is all about," gesturing with his hand to indicate the hundreds of people scattered about. "Was there an accident?"

The man removed his pipe from his mouth, exhaling a cherry scented tobacco into the air about him. He paused a few seconds to evaluate Igor in his car before responding. "You must be from out of town." He tapped his wife with an elbow to the ribs. "The President is flying in here in about 30 minutes. The crowd you refer to is the welcoming committee." The man placed his pipe back in his mouth, shaking his head at Igor before leading his wife by the hand, trying to get a better vantage point as he moved with the pack.

Igor realized he was on the right track. He was absolutely sure of it. If the roles had been reversed, it's what he would have done.

The clock was ticking—he had 30 minutes to prevent a nightmare from happening.

A five-meter long wood bridge led to Fort Mifflin's sole entrance, echoing Peter's heavy footsteps as he crossed. The bridge itself stood over a four-meter wide moat that looked to dependant on the generosity of the Delaware Rivers tide to provide the Forts protection, currently exposing its muddy bottom. *Hate to slip in there,* he thought, careful to avoid its steep banks. Looking up at the Revolutionary War era Forts imposing brick structure then from side-to-side, Peter noticed that it was built in a pentagonal shape similar to a brick structure that was located outside of his hometown of Sergov.

The Forts massive wooden doors were locked and bolted for the night, providing some sense of reassurance to Peter. The last thing he needed was some unsuspecting soul lurking on the Forts exterior. He knew the guards would only worry about its treasured interior. So he should be safe on the outside. Peter followed the narrow dirt footpath that ran between the Fort and its moat, allowing it to lead him to where the Forts brick façade turned into an earthen wall of the about the same height. The earthen wall was originally built to withstand enemy ships cannon blasts, absorbing the cannon balls in its soft, ruddy earth so they couldn't penetrate to the forts interior.

The Forts earthen edge was located a mere 20 meters from the banks of the Delaware Rivers. Suitably for Peter, this would also be his starting point. Looking from side-to-side for his bearings, Peter positioned himself on the Forts southwestern corner. He walked in a straight line five meters from the forts edge, pacing off the distance as he walked towards both the moat and the river. Peter could see and feel a minor depression in the earth where he stopped counting off his steps, two-meters from the edge of the moat. *This is it,* he said excitedly eyeing his watch to make sure he was still on schedule. Satisfied he still had plenty of time, he placed the shovel into the soft ground to remove the first spade full of earth.

From his perch above the Forts earthen wall, Tom Giacono sat on his rocker, gazing between pleasure craft heading in for the night and the majestic sunset. *What a fantastic day to be alive,* hoping his wife had the same view from their homes back porch. *Where else could I actually get paid to work and have a view like this?* He looked at his watch before rising up from his rocker in order to perform his hourly rounds.

Stretching his legs due to his sitting so long, Tom tried to work out a leg cramp. He jogged in place for several moments to no avail. He should have listened to his wife and taken some potassium pills. Damn if she wasn't right again. Deciding it was best just to walk it off. Moving towards the edge of the Forts earthen edge, he heard a sharp metallic noise somewhere below. It sounded as if someone were digging and had struck a rock.

Tom had been warned by his supervisor about history buffs who scoured the grounds around historic battle sites with metal detectors, searching for items of value to sell to collectors on e-bay, hoping to make a quick buck or two.

Tom walked to the Forts earthen edge to view over the wall, careful not to lose his footing and avoid a 20-foot drop. With a clear, unobstructed view all the way to the river, he was afforded an excellent vantage point. Looking both ways he could see nothing as the sun's light faded into night. Having also heard numerous accounts of ghost soldiers coming back to visit the place of their deaths, Tom discounted those stories as "hogwash," for the tourists. No, he had definitely heard something close-by and it was not a figment of his imagination nor supernatural in nature. Walking the remaining 50 feet over to the western side of the Fort, he leaned over where the brick edge met the earthen portion of the Fort. He scanned from north to south, peering into the night's twilight when he heard yet another sharp metallic click. This time it was off to his left, enabling him to narrow the focus of his search to a specific area. His eyes getting older and not being what they were 50 years before, it took time for Tom to notice movement below him and towards the edge of the moat. Focusing more intently on the shadowy figure before him, he could see it was a man digging in a pit, a pile of dirt in evidence beside him. Tom backed away from the edge not wanting to alarm the man. He instinctively reached for his 38 caliber, Smith & Wesson snub nose, opening its barrel and inserting six bullets from his pocket where they were mixed with his spare change. Tom always carried the weapon empty, trying to avoid an accidental shooting if he tripped or fell.

Quickly making his way down the forts interior steps, Tom maneuvered carefully among the Forts stationary displays, making his way to the Forts only entrance and exit, the front gate.

Sliding back the 200-year old lock which essentially employed a six foot wooden beam as its main deterrent, Tom was able to crack open the door to peer outside. He looked from side-to-side to see if there was a lookout in place, having heard during training lectures that they usually operated in pairs. Observing the illuminated parking lot off to his right, he spied another car beside his own. *He even had the nerve to park beside me!*

Slipping through the open door, Tom pulled it shut as best he could. Carefully maneuvering up the Forts living history trail to where he last saw the shadow of a man digging, fingering his weapon as he walked. Tom was ready, nervous, but ready.

The digging proceeded at a fairly rapid pace with the ground still soft from the previous night's rain. The soils content had the consistently of a good Irish peat moss, with the dirt lifting up as though it had wings attached to it. After 60 minutes of digging, his shovel struck something metallic, a hollow ping its announcement. He excitedly tossed aside the shovel, looking up at the Forts ramparts to see if anyone else had overheard the sound. Sensing no movement, Peter resumed digging, only now with his calloused hands. He had no desire to damage the suitcase's exterior with the metal shovel.

An additional five minutes of simply moving the soft earth aside provided him with the outline of a suitcase, digging along its sides until he was able to locate its titanium handle. A smile crept across his face as he yanked the case from its earthen grave. The very case that was first placed there by a KGB agent some 35 years earlier, an excitement crept through Peter as if a child opening presents on Christmas Day. Placing the case beside his freshly dug pile of earth he noticed a wire attached to the unit; he pulled on the buried wire and it immediately gave way. Peter realized it must be the power source. *Of course it couldn't just stay buried underground*, he thought, *it required some form of energy to function.* He instinctively checked his watch to see that he still had 20 minutes until the president's aircraft landed. If he could set the weapon and arrange the timer to explode in 15 minutes, he could still manage to escape. The president would still be in the process of greeting various dignitaries on the airports tarmac, this before heading downtown for his speech at Philadelphia's prestigious Union Club.

But if Peter ran out of time and could not escape, he would become a martyr to his people.

Negotiating the crowd was slow at best until a police officer took pity on seeing Igor's car surrounded by a sea of people swarming his auto from both sides. The officer waded into the crowd blowing his whistle as he went, able to clear a path for his car, allowing him to proceed on his way. Igor provided a casual salute to the officer in response as he drove past, thanking him for the kind gesture.

Once past the anxious crowd, Igor drove the remaining two kilometers to the Forts entrance. The road was devoid of traffic with everyone concentrating on the President's arrival. Turning off his cars headlights before he turned into the Forts entrance, he didn't need a potential lookout to identify him. With this in mind, he wisely chose to park just off the airport's perimeter road and out of view. Igor would walk the last hundred meters or so. It would provide him with a chance to reconnoiter the lay of the land, always important before any assault. Exiting his car, he proceeded to his trunk and his arsenal, removing two grenades, night vision goggles and his 9mm. He was ready for battle.

Jogging down past the Forts parking lot, he approached a wooden bridge that crossed the Fort's moat. Stopping to scout the immediate area before realizing he had no other options, he slowly made his way across by softly sliding his feet, realizing the sounds of his crossing would echo off the wood for 50 meters or so if he walked normally. Once across, he knelt on the grass to scan both directions around the Fort for any signs of activity. Satisfied he was indeed alone, he donned his night vision gear, adjusting its intensity and once again scouring the Forts perimeter before proceeding. With his night vision gear, the night's darkness would be his ally. Looking straight ahead, he detected the main door to the Fort ajar. That presented him with two options: that the security guard was on patrol and carelessly left the door open or the rebel was now in the Fort using it as a platform for his mission. Igor prayed for the first option.

Following Sergey's directions he readied his weapon before proceeding down the path between the moat and the Fort.

It was time.

Using the base of a 30 foot oak tree for cover, well within range of the person who was digging, Tom took several deep breaths to calm his racing nerves, looking up to the sky and wondering what in the hell he was getting himself into. Looking down to his weapon, he stepped out from behind the tree, pointing his weapon at the man that stood before him.

"Freeze," mimicking the same stern tone he heard Police use on the television. "Stop the digging and put your hands in the air!"

Peter was caught completely off-guard, being so engrossed in his work that he had disregarded his immediate surroundings. *Damn you.* Having been instructed to always stay in synch with the area in which you work. Searching the night's darkness in the general area from where the voice had emanated, his hawk-like eyes locating the man's distinctive shadow outline a short distance away. Peter cursed aloud, realizing his own weapon lay just of reach, located halfway between himself and his newfound friend. He had removed it from his pants waistband in order to dig more freely, without constrictions, this being his second possibly fatal mistake.

"To whom do I owe the pleasure of meeting?" Peter said, trying to draw the man closer and possibly overwhelm him or at least stall for time, enabling him to dive for his own weapon.

Moving closer to his subject, Tom flicked on his bulky flashlight, shining it sharply in Peters face, still pointing his weapon at the man.

"Don't try any funny business. I have a weapon here and I know how to use it, son," Tom said menacingly. He looked down at the metal case Peter had recently removed. "What do we have here?" He then pointed down at the case with the flashlight's beam. "Does this help you detect metal items in the ground that you then dig up and steal from the American people? Looks like a fancy metal detector."

Peter's mind raced before realizing the man had unwittingly provided him an excuse for his being there. The security guard must be thinking that he was stealing wartime related artifacts from the hallowed grounds surrounding the fort. That had to be his rationale. Only now to play along with that very thought.

"You caught me, sir," Peter said. He was trying to find a foothold that would enable him to spring from the hole and dive for his weapon. "I have found something of extreme importance and placed it in this case for transport. I was hoping to sell it for close to a million dollars. He was trying to pique Tom's interest and have him to move closer to the case, knowing he couldn't balance both the gun and the flashlight at the same time. Something would have to give.

"And I already have a buyer."

The flashlight almost dropped from his hand when he heard the man say one million dollars. That would supplement a lot of vacation time thought Tom, as he stood there dumbfounded. He had to lean against a tree for some stability in order to keep from falling down.

"Are you telling me,........Do you mean,........," Tom said, stammering as he searched for the proper words. "You dug something up around here that was worth one million dollars?" His senses grabbed hold, wondering what this guy was trying to pull, his hand tightening on the gun. "Now wait one minute, young man."

"Look for yourself," Peter said. He directed his attention back towards the metal case. Peter had to move quickly, this man was having some doubts about the credibility of his story. He could tell he wasn't dealing with the typical stereotyped security guard, uneducated and bored with the job. That type of person would have called in the police to handle his intruding upon the forts property. This man had ambitions. But he also was aware of the predicament that all security guards in the US faced, undervalued and underpaid. Underlining that issue could work to his advantage and where Peter could strike first. Money.

"If you were to over look this little incident, I may see my way to providing you a 10% finder's fee." He knew he had the security guards full attention, as Peter found a foothold and was ready to maneuver closer to his weapon, waiting for the right moment.

Tom's mind was spinning now. *A hundred grand just for looking the other way?* Several moments passed as Tom stood transfixed staring at the case; the money already spent supplementing the little extras in life he and his wife would require. He looked back in time to see Peter trying to extract himself from the earthen hole.

"Stop right there," Tom said, common sense taking hold, moving the flashlight over to the metal case then back to

Peter. "What's to stop me from taking the case and making the deal myself, that way I get to keep the whole million?"

Peter realized he now possessed the man's soul. He had snapped at the bait.

"You're right, you could have the whole million. But you would also require the buyers information now wouldn't you? Peter had attained his position and ready to dive for his weapon. "Let me call the buyer right now," pointing over to where the case was, possibly leading the man to think he had a cell phone near the case. "He doesn't live far from here."

Everything was moving way too quickly for Tom. Walking closer to both Peter and the case, realizing he held the edge with a loaded weapon to back him up. "All right, I'll take the 10%," Tom said against his better judgment, something deep inside telling him that everything wasn't as cut and dry as it seemed. "But you have to fill in this hole," using his flashlight to point to the 3-foot deep hole Peter stood in.

The Americans and their greed had saved him once more from certain death. That was the one surefire downfall for most Americans, greed. Only money talks in their capitalist society.

"Deal," Peter replied, having nothing to lose, knowing there was no money or artifact in his case to sell, only its lure. "Can I get out from this hole without you shooting me?"

"One minute," Tom said, "Catch," throwing the flashlight to Peter. "You hold the flashlight so I can open the case. That way I still have my gun pointed at you," thinking he had outsmarted the thief with his simple maneuver. "I want to see what a million dollars looks like," fumbling with the cases titanium latches.

Peter caught the flashlight with one hand. The idiot having provided him a weapon: one lacking bullets but still a weapon.

"Thank-you for your trust," Peter said sarcastically, holding the flashlight, its beam redirected on the case. "Go ahead, open it," looking over at his own weapon only a meter away.

The helicopter that Michael Forsythe and his team *appropriated* happened to be one of the Navy's latest Seahawk's, fresh from the Sikorsky manufacturing line and delivered only a week earlier. Coming straight off the manufacturing line, it still lacked any of its associated weaponry or anti-submarine avionics, providing additional room for Forsythe, Thomson, and Rocco to ride along in relative comfort.

Luckily for Forsythe the helicopter was on a flight training exercise out of Patuxent River Naval Air Station and operating in nearby airspace when ordered to Washington DC. It landed on the Washington mall within 30 minutes of the FBI helicopter being stolen and took off within seconds of Forsythe's team boarding.

Flying the helicopter was newly minted Navy Lieutenant Anson West and Commander Alison Half. Being fresh out of Navy helicopter flight school, Lieutenant West required 155 hours of flight time before he could be considered qualified to be a Seahawk pilot in charge.

Due to the unforeseen circumstances, the helicopter and its pilots both operated under the command of Forsythe, those on direct orders of the Joint Chiefs of Staff, they having been recently briefed on the weapons existence.

Forsythe provided the pilots with their new priority, allowing them to put the helicopters advertised speed to the test. Hopefully they would arrive in time to prevent a potential disaster from unraveling.

With the Presidents aircraft, Air Force One, already alerted to the emerging situation, it was diverted to Andrews Air Force Base. The base also contained an emergency bunker which was built in the 1950's to withstand a direct, low-grade, nuclear attack and was now being put to use as the nations new command post until the event passed.

Forsythe had alerted the FBI's Philadelphia office while in-route to the situation and ordered his fellow agents to clear the immediate area surrounding the Fort. He also informed them that they were not to approach anywhere within one mile of the Fort itself. That prize was to be reserved for himself and his ad hoc team. They would take the suspect down.

"Sir, we are approaching the Philadelphia International Airport," said the Navy Commander as she pointed out the pulsing white runway lights just ahead. "We have been given complete control of the Philadelphia Airspace by the airports control tower, sir. It's your call."

"Commander, proceed down to the far eastern edge of the airport where we are supposed to have a car waiting for us," Forsythe said, removing his weapon and checking its status, indicating for Jim and Rocco to do the same.

"It's time, gentlemen. Lock and load."

The night vision gear was an ideal asset for Igor as he maneuvered the Forts manicured dirt trail, careful to avoid the moats muddy bank on his right-hand side. He had his weapon positioned in front of him, ready for any unforeseen dangers as he approached what appeared to be a sharp turn in the Forts structure. Positioning himself flat against the Forts thick brick wall, he was able to peer around its edge with his awkward head mounted gear, not wanting to be surprised by anyone on the other side. Taking a quick 5-second glimpse, Igor was able to view two men, one with a flashlight standing above another man in an apparent hole no more than 20 meters away.

So I see he has help, Igor thought, peering once again around the wall, this time for a few seconds more. With him able to clearly see the area around him and any potential pitfalls that the terrain provided, Igor decided to make his way towards the figures position. Luckily for him, Igor was able to view the figures clearly due to the subject's flashlight providing the illumination source for his night vision gear, enhancing the view usually relied upon the moons light to provide daylight viewing conditions.

Carefully maneuvering close enough to overhear the men's conversation involving money and a metal case, Igor realized he had acquired his rebel. The chase was about to reach a climatic end. The other man with him was apparently a newfound accomplice or quite possibly a buyer, not that it mattered for they were both about to meet their respective God. This was not a situation where prisoners are to be accorded the rights of the Geneva Convention.

Igor took advantage of the animated discussion to quietly approach his subjects, positioning himself behind an old oak tree for security, fixing his weapon on the uniformed man standing over the hole.

Taking a deep breath, Igor readied for battle once more, before announcing himself. "If you would both stop what you are doing, I can remove that case you are arguing over and be on my way."

The security guard was caught off balance from the unexpected appearance of the person behind him, turning quickly in response to the intrusion, his weapon making the turn before his body.

Igor had no choice but to shoot before the man chose to shoot first, able to squeeze off one quick shot from his weapon, the bullet entered Tom's chest cavity, killing him instantly and the momentum tossing his body rearward towards Peter. Unfortunately, the sudden flash from Igor's weapon temporarily blinded him due to his night vision gear magnifying any light source. It was as if a flashbulb had just illuminated directly in his eyes.

With the weapons sudden discharge, Peter saw an opportunity to take advantage of the situation and retrieve his own weapon. Searching the murky darkness, Peter located it opposite his shovel. Quickly retrieving it and rolling back into the hole he had dug, removing the safety. The area's sudden popularity was starting to alarm Peter as he lay with his back braced against the fresh earthen wall, ready to repel the new invader.

Igor removed the night vision headgear, throwing the delicate electronic piece carelessly to the ground, blinking several times in a fight to clear his vision of the effects of the guns sudden flash. Feeling foolish, he of all people should have realized the blinding effects provided by the weapon's discharge on the night vision gear. Standing out in the open, he suddenly realized he was a sitting duck, falling flat to the ground, his weapon pointing towards where he had last saw Peter.

Peter was trapped. That much he realized. His immediate choices were fast appearing grim. The hole he had just dug was now taking on some resemblance of a grave. If this newcomer had any company with him, they could easily surround Peter's position due to the Forts wall being on one side and the river on the other. There was only one chance of escape—Peter had to kill whoever was out there. Leaning out of his hole, Peter fired a shot in the general direction of the man in front of him, the shot echoing loudly through the night's air. At least that might delay a charge towards his somewhat defensible position—with the outsider now realizing he was armed.

Igor instinctively ducked his head, hugging the ground even more if it were possible, the bullet ricocheting off the Forts brick wall before embedding into the dirt in front of him. Peter aimed his own 9mm and placed a shot into the pile of dirt in front of Peter, the weapons noise being the only sound in the darkness besides the whirling blades of a helicopter landing somewhere off in the distance.

"Why don't you give up and come out with your hands up, surrender before I have to kill you," Igor yelled, hoping he wasn't killed himself by some errant bullet.

Looking to his left, Peter could see that the Titanium case was easily within his arms reach. He could pull it into the hole and code the weapon for an immediate detonation. That would enable him to still accomplish his mission. He would die a martyr's death.

Looking to the east, Peter realized the time had come. Positioning himself for a rapid two shot burst to keep the other man off guard—Peter leaned up and out of his hole, firing before grabbing the case, sliding it onto his lap. *This would be his grave.*

Igor was ready, knowing the type of criminal he was dealing with. He was a fanatic. The two shot burst caused Igor to dive for the exposed ground, waiting until Peter had pulled the suitcase into the hole, knowing he would be slightly off balance by the case's sudden weight. This could work to Igor's advantage. Jumping up from his position, Igor ran the remaining five meters up to the dirt pile, diving at its base causing some of the dirt to fall in on Peter who now couldn't turn around or get up due to the suitcase being on his lap. Igor then reached over the top with his weapon and fired two shots of his own into the hole, not worried about hitting and damaging the weapon due to its protective titanium case.

Igor waited several seconds before repeating the motion. He then rolled around the dirt pile with his empty weapon still fixed on where he expected Peter to be, seeing Peter to the left of where he had anticipated, Peter now pointing his weapon at him.

"Goodbye," shouted Peter, shooting Igor in the face. "Allah Akbar."

He reached over to grab the security guards' still lit flashlight, prying it from his dead hands. Peter then pulled the suitcase up and out of the pit he had dug. He had his own schedule to meet.

Using the security guards flashlight he was able to snap open the clasps and then the units' lid. A smile graced his face as he pushed the toggle switch to on, engaging the weapon, its dials lighting up and showing full power on its gauge. He quickly entered the suitcases code number, the unit making a humming noise in response. Peter smiled once more, this time shouting "Allah Akbar."

"Did you hear that?" Forsythe said in a hushed tone.

Rocco and Jim instinctively dove for cover outside the Forts front entrance, the popping noise sounding as if a string of firecrackers had been set off.

Rocco was first to respond. "Definitely 9mm shots."

Jim was next. "It sounded like it came from the footpath."

"From the information we have on the Forts layout, this is the only way out," Forsythe said. "We'll stay here and take him or them when they emerge."

Forsythe removed his own 9mm Beretta from his leather shoulder holster.

"Rocco you take the first shot," he ordered, knowing that Rocco had a night scope mounted on his weapon. *He also wouldn't miss.*

"Roger that boss," Rocco replied, flipping around his black baseball cap so it wouldn't interfere with his shot.

Forsythe watched as his men expertly dispersed across the trail without so much as an order from him, taking up positions exactly where he would have placed them.

Experts all.

Peter sat looking at his watch. He had missed his deadline by two minutes. No matter. He could still accomplish his mission. He chose to silently pray to the east and Mecca.

Rocco was the first to speak. "Boss, it's been five minutes; we have to check out what's going on down that path."

Forsythe was the first to move forward, Rocco just behind him. "All right let's go."

Rocco held his weapons stock squarely against his shoulder as he surveyed the scene through its night vision scope, walking down the dirt path, wanting to verify the spot was right where Boris had said the weapon would be. They could not have another weapon on the loose.

Peter heard a noise off towards the parking lot. He instinctively switched off the flashlight. The Devil's Suitcase was ready. He only had to push the red button and he would become a Martyr.

"Did you see that?" asked Rocco, having seen the flashlight switch off.

Forsythe nodded. "If you have a shot take it," he said as silently as he could muster.

"Will do. I have to move forward to clear the dirt he has piled in front of him."

Forsythe had his gun leading the way as he moved closer, Rocco now off to his left.

Peter smiled as the agents moved closer. "I will choose the time we all shall die," he murmured. He once again looked to the suitcase then to the approaching agents.

Using his night scope, Rocco was in a better position to see what Peter was up to. "Boss, he has the nuke suitcase on his lap, finger on what appears to be the button."

"Take the damn shot," Forsythe screamed.

At the same moment Peter heard Forsythe yell to take the shot, he screamed "Allah Akbar," pushing down on the suitcases button just as Rocco's bullet entered his head.

CHAPTER TWENTY-SIX

Washington DC

The president was moved from Andrews Air Force Base back to the White House Secure Room, eight stories beneath the White House. The National Security Advisor thought it best for the President to back in the Nation's Capital instead of being accused of running from a lone terrorist.

A lone terrorist with a nuclear weapon.

The National Security Advisor said he had to look *Presidential* to the nation.

The Red Phone beeped at the end of the conference table. The Presidents military aide quickly picked it up. He listened for the caller's authentication code. "Sir, we have a situation," he said before handing the phone to the President. The President listened for several seconds before dropping the phone to the floor, shock spreading across his face. The Chief of the Joint Chiefs of Staff looked to the President before he grabbed the phone, listening to the rest of the conversation; he then placed it on speaker for all to hear. "Colonel, please repeat what you just told the President and myself."

"Yes, Sir. Approximately twenty minutes ago we detected a nuclear explosion in the southwest section of Philadelphia. We are currently estimating a shock wave that progressed to a point three miles ahead of the explosion. The explosion resulting in initial estimates of between 150,000 to 200,000 killed, possibly another 50,000 from radiation in the coming months. The first satellite pass shows the International airport, two local refineries, and the residential areas surrounding both completely destroyed."

The President shook his head as tears suddenly appeared, streaking down his cheeks."

The Chief of the Joint Chiefs of Staff thanked the caller before he hung up.

"How many more of these are on our soil," he shouted at the CIA representative.

"We think between 25 to 30, sir," she replied timidly. "But we really don't have an exact number. We have about the same number on Russian soil, sir."

The President shook off his initial reaction. "Get me the Russian Premier," he demanded. "I want every single one of our nuclear suitcases off Russian soil; and they get theirs off our soil. If they chose to deny what just happened, we will detonate one of ours near Moscow. This stops today, people."

Russian officials reversed their earlier position and finally admitted to the existence of suitcase nuclear weapons having been in the Russian Military inventory for over 40 years. They went on to state that the weapons were being withdrawn from service for eventual destruction under cognizance of a committee composed of Russian Military officials with assistance from an unnamed foreign country.

The group was to be under the leadership of Russian General Poszk.

Several days later, the British foreign ministry admitted that they had undertaken and financed a deal with the Russian government to remove and destroy all of its small portable nuclear weapons.

The British had selected Sir Robert John to assist the committee as their representative.

Within months, with twenty-nine weapons identified and destroyed, the committee was disbanded with much fanfare, having accomplished a great service to mankind.

Only one problem still existed; General Poszk and Sir Robert John had destroyed only twenty-nine—one was still missing.........

THE END

Amazon Best Selling author Francis Joseph Smith has traveled to most of the world during his tenure in the Armed Forces (Navy & Air Force) and as an Analyst for an unnamed Government Agency, providing him with numerous fictional plot lines and settings for future use. His experiences provide readers with well researched, fast-paced action. Smith's novels are the result of years of preparation to become a fiction writer in the genre of Clancy, Griffin, Higgins, and Cussler.

Smith lives with his family in a small town outside of Philadelphia where he is currently in work on his next novel.

Made in the USA
Middletown, DE
15 April 2019